The Amish Christmas Cowboy

Jo Ann Brown

H HARLEQUIN® LOVE INSPIRED®

Recycling programs for this product may not exist in your area.

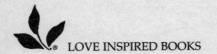

LOVE INSPIRED BOOKS

ISBN-13: 978-1-335-50976-5

The Amish Christmas Cowboy

Copyright © 2018 by Jo Ann Ferguson

www.Harlequin.com

Printed in U.S.A.

And the multitude of them that believed
were of one heart and of one soul:
neither said any of them that ought of
the things which he possessed was his own;
but they had all things common.
—*Acts* 4:32

For Melissa Endlich.
Thank you for making me feel so welcome
in the Love Inspired family.

Chapter One

Harmony Creek Hollow, New York

"Guess what, Sarah?"

The last thing Sarah Kuhns wanted to do was play a guessing game with Natalie Summerhays, the oldest of the four *kinder* in the house where Sarah worked as the nanny. At ten, Natalie was poised partway between being a *kind* and standing on the precipice of becoming a teenager.

"What?" Sarah asked as she wondered why anyone with small *kinder* would build a house with columns within a youngster's reach from the bannister on the staircase curving above the elegant entry's marble floors. She'd talked four-year-old Mia into letting Sarah pluck her off one fluted column. Ethan, who at five years old considered himself invulnerable, wasn't willing to give up his attempt to touch the ceiling twenty feet above the floor.

God, grant me patience, she prayed as she did often while watching the Summerhays *kinder*. *Please let this be the last time I have to save these little ones from their antics. At least for today...*

Motioning with her hands, she called to Ethan again, *"Komm, kind."*

His head jerked around, and he grinned as the *kinder* often did when she spoke to them in *Deitsch*. For some reason, they found the words she used at home funny. She had no idea why.

Ethan's blond hair fell into his blue eyes, and he reached to push it aside. With a yelp, he began to slide down the column.

Sarah leaned over the bannister, praying it wouldn't collapse or her glasses wouldn't slip off and crash to the floor. She caught the little boy's shirt as he dropped past her. He shrieked, and she wrapped her fingers in the fabric. With a big jerk that resonated through her shoulders, she flipped him across the rail and into her arms. The motion knocked her from her feet, and she sat hard on a step.

Her heart hammered against her ribs as she held the little boy close. He shook, and she cuddled him to her. Maybe he understood how he could have been hurt.

Then she realized he was laughing! He thought the whole thing had been fun. When he squirmed to get out of her hold, she tightened it.

She felt sorry for the four *kinder* who always were looking for ways to be noticed. Their parents were busy—Mr. Summerhays with his businesses and his racehorses and Mrs. Summerhays redoing her wardrobe and the house every two to three months—and they paid little attention to their kids. Even when one or more acted outrageously, the mischief seldom registered with their busy parents.

Carrying Ethan down the stairs while leading Mia by the hand, Sarah said, "You told me you wouldn't climb the columns again."

"We didn't climb them," Mia said with the aplomb

of a four-year-old attorney arguing a legal loophole in a courtroom. "We got on them up there."

Sarah resisted rolling her eyes as she put Ethan on his feet. The youngsters nitpicked everything. In the nine months since she'd taken the job as nanny, she'd learned to be specific when setting parameters for them. Apparently, she hadn't been specific enough.

How her friends in the Harmony Creek Spinsters' Club would laugh when she told them about this! They were getting together that evening to attend the second annual Berry-fest Dinner to benefit the local volunteer fire department. She wondered if her friends had guessed that she told them less than a quarter of the "adventures" her charges got into each day. She tried to head the *kinder* off before they were hurt, but didn't want to hover over them. Being overprotective wasn't *gut* for anyone. She knew that too well.

"Sarah!" Natalie stamped her foot. "Did you hear me?"

"Just a minute." Frowning at the younger *kinder*, she ordered, "No more getting on the columns anywhere."

"From floor to ceiling?" asked Ethan.

"And everywhere in between. No getting on the columns. Understood?"

Ethan and Mia glanced at each other, then nodded.

"Sarah!" Natalie crossed her arms over her bright red T-shirt. "Sarah, are you listening?"

Watching the two little ones skipping across the fancy rug that cost more than the farm where she lived with her two brothers, Sarah sighed. She faced the impatient ten-year-old who'd inherited her *mamm's* glistening black hair and gray eyes. Someday, Natalie would be a beauty like her *mamm*, but with her lips compressed, she looked like the *kind* she was.

"I'm listening." Sarah smoothed her black apron that

had gotten bunched against her dark green dress when she'd kept Ethan from falling. For a moment, she wondered what Alexander, the fourth Summerhays youngster, was up to. She would check once she listened to Natalie. Checking her *kapp* was in place, she asked, "What's up, Natalie?"

"Did someone order a cowboy?"

Stunned, she stared at the girl. "Why would you ask me that?"

"Because there are cowboys on the porch."

She struggled not to frown. The *kinder* had played plenty of pranks on her when she first began working for Mr. and Mrs. Summerhays. Childish practical jokes like a whoopee cushion beneath her and spiders in her glass. She'd laughed along with them, until they'd stopped. Or she'd thought they had.

When she'd been offered the job, she'd seen it as a gift from God. It provided her with an open window into *Englisch* lives, allowing her to learn what she'd need to know if she decided to move away from the Harmony Creek settlement. Her stomach clenched. She didn't want to leave her brothers or the *wunderbaar* friends she'd made since they moved to northern New York last year, but being baptized meant surrendering her dream of helping others.

That dream had been born the day she went to visit her *daed* in the hospital after a serious barn accident. He'd lost his right arm, and she guessed he might have given up if it hadn't been for the nurses and physical therapists who'd believed in him. Watching them, she'd decided she wanted to learn to do such work, but that would be impossible if she became a full member of the Amish church. However, a job like a volunteer EMT might be allowed.

"Natalie," she began.

"There are cowboys out there!" insisted the girl. "If you don't believe me, look for yourself."

Sarah took a quick glance at the top of the wide door to make sure someone hadn't rigged a bucket of water on it. The fancy door was hinged in the middle, and she kept a close eye on the other side…just in case. The August heat battered her like an open oven door.

"See?" demanded Natalie.

Lowering her gaze from the door's top, Sarah gasped when she saw who stood on the wide porch.

A cowboy!

A real live cowboy!

She stared in disbelief at his wide-brimmed straw hat that looked as if it'd been plucked out of one of her brother Menno's Zane Grey novels. Though the day was warm, he wore a long-sleeved light green shirt and denims. His black Western boots had scuffed toes. Sun-streaked brown hair fell forward into the bluest eyes she'd ever seen, bluer than a cloudless summer sky.

"Ma'am, is this Ian Summerhays's place?" asked another cowboy, who tipped his black hat as he came up the steps. He was older, old enough to be her *daed*, and his slow drawl came, she guessed, right out of the heart of Texas.

"*Ja*... Yes, it is." She couldn't pull her gaze from the younger man, who gaped at her in outright astonishment.

Hadn't he seen a plain woman before? If he hadn't, he should still have known it wasn't polite to stare.

Then, realizing she was doing the same, she cut her eyes to the older man and asked, "Are you looking for Mr. Summerhays?"

"Is he around?"

"He's in his office." She didn't add how rare that was.

He spent most days at the stables in Saratoga, about an hour's drive south.

"Can you let him know we've got a delivery for him?" The older man gestured toward a large truck with a massive horse trailer behind it.

South Texas Stables was written on the side of the trailer in fading red letters. Through the narrow windows, motions revealed animals were inside. She was relieved to hear the sound of an air-conditioning unit coming on, knowing the animals would be more comfortable than she was in her bed on a hot summer night when the air was still.

"Of course." She turned to Natalie. "Please go and let your *daed* know there's a delivery."

The little girl glanced at the men on the porch and, for a moment, Sarah thought she would protest.

Natalie grinned. "I told you there were cowboys out here."

"You did." Bending, Sarah said, "Mrs. Beebe said she was going to have a treat for you this afternoon." The cook knew the youngsters were always ready for a snack. "You can check with her if it's ready after you let your *daed* know someone wants to talk with him."

"Okay, I get it. You want to talk to the cowboy by yourself. Don't let him sweep you onto his horse and ride off with you into the sunset." She giggled before running inside.

Sarah hoped neither man had heard the girl. Those hopes were dashed when she aimed a furtive look in the younger man's direction and saw his frown. His light brown brows were lowered like storm clouds over his bright blue eyes. Intense emotion filled them, but she didn't know why he was distressed.

After Natalie had rushed away to her *daed's* office

in the left wing of the house, Sarah looked at the men, unsure what to say next. She wished Mrs. Summerhays were there, but the *kinder's mamm* was in Europe, buying items in antiques shops in Paris and Rome and Vienna to create her new vision for the house. Should Sarah ask the two men in? No, three men. Another guy with a cowboy hat walked around the trailer. Leaning against it, the dark-haired man lit a cigarette, startling her. Mr. Summerhays didn't like anyone smoking near the house or stables.

Her face must have revealed that, because the older man snapped an order at the third cowboy. With a grimace, he dropped the cigarette and ground it out with the toe of his boot.

"Sorry, ma'am," said the older man. "Ned forgets his manners sometimes." He aimed a frown at the man by the trailer.

Wanting to put an end to the uncomfortable conversation, Sarah asked, "Was Mr. Summerhays expecting you?"

"We're a day early, but I warned him we might be. By the way, I'm J.J. Rafferty, and that talkative guy there—" he pointed at the younger man who hadn't said a word "—is Toby Christner. Toby, show the lady that you can talk."

"Nice to meet you," the handsome cowboy said. His baritone voice would have been pleasant on the ear if he'd put inflection in it.

"I'm Sarah Kuhns," she answered.

J.J. nodded toward her, then looked past her.

Sarah turned to see Natalie standing behind her. "Did you talk to your *daed*?"

The girl nodded. "He'll be out in a few minutes. He's finishing a call."

"We'll catch up on a few things," J.J. said, "while we're waiting." He walked toward the truck, motioning for Ned to follow him.

The dark-haired man winked at her before going with J.J.

Toby remained where he was. So did his frown. What was bothering him? Was he upset Mr. Summerhays hadn't dropped everything to greet them when they arrived? If they'd done business with her boss, they should have known how busy he was. So busy he seldom came home before ten, long after the *kinder* were tucked into bed. He was gone at dawn to the stables in Saratoga or to New York City, where he did something there with the stock market.

Sarah wished she could think of something to say to the tall man who didn't seem in a hurry to join the others. She'd gotten comfortable talking with *Englischers* since she started working as a nanny. Something about the man's posture told her engaging him in small talk would be futile. She was curious how many horses were being delivered to the stables, but held her tongue.

J.J. and Ned returned to the porch after a few minutes. If they'd come to the house she shared with her two brothers deep in the hollow with Harmony Creek at its center, she'd know what to do. She would have brought them into the kitchen and asked them to sit at the table while she served iced tea and chilled pie.

Should she do the same here? She couldn't invite them into the kitchen. Mrs. Summerhays had her guests brought to the room she called the library, though there weren't any books in it. Sarah wished the housekeeper were here, but it was Mrs. Hancock's day off. Mrs. Beebe, the cook, had her hands full with getting meals ready while the kitchen was being renovated…again. It was the third time in two years Mrs. Summerhays had decided it needed a complete updating.

Knowing she must not leave the men standing on the porch in the heat, she said, "Please *komm* inside where you can wait for Mr. Summerhays."

Toby cleared his throat. "I can—"

"Come along, both of you," said J.J. "I don't want to unload the horses until Summerhays checks them to make sure they meet his satisfaction. We had a tough enough time getting the bay into the trailer the first time. He'll be more resolute not to go in again."

"But—"

"No sense standing out in the heat. Any chance you might have something cool to drink, young lady?"

"I'm sure there's something. I can check."

"Much obliged." J.J. motioned for her to go ahead of him, then followed her into the large entry along with Toby and Ned. As J.J. took his hat off, he gave a low whistle. "Mighty fine spread here."

She hadn't heard anyone talk like him before but guessed he was complimenting the house. She had a lot to learn about *Englischers*. Finding out about *Englisch* ways was going to be a bigger task than she'd guessed.

"I'll find out what's on ice in the kitchen." She shouldn't leave them in the entry, but she wasn't sure where to take them. Mrs. Beebe would know what to do, because the cook had been working at the house since the family moved in.

"Whatever you've got will be great," J.J. said.

She smiled in return, then spun and hurried toward the kitchen. She glanced back. Her gaze was caught by the younger man, who regarded her with the same expressionless look.

How odd! At that moment, she would have given a penny to know his thoughts. Maybe even two.

The last person Toby Christner had expected would answer the door was an Amish woman. If someone had warned him ahead of time, he would have thought it was a joke. She wasn't any more out of place in the fancy house than the house itself was among the other simple farms they'd seen along the road toward the Vermont border. Stone pillars by the road were set next to a fancy sign announcing Summerhays Stables, which lay beyond them. The whole setup matched the prestige Ian Summerhays was garnering with his excellent racehorses, including the three his boss had brought from Texas, where Toby had been working with them for a year.

He glanced at the young Amish woman, who was rushing away as if she couldn't wait to be done with them. Not that he blamed her. Ned Branigan hadn't stopped trying to get her attention. Toby wanted to tell his coworker his sly wiles wouldn't work on an Amish woman, but Ned would have ignored him.

Sarah wasn't tall. In fact, when he'd moved closer to her to go inside, she'd taken a step back so she didn't have to tilt her head to look at him. She had bright red hair beneath her *kapp*. Her gold-rimmed glasses hadn't been able to hide the surprise in her mahogany-brown eyes when she'd seen him on the porch.

Toby let his boss and Ned lead the way into the magnificent house. It was grander than the house on J.J.'s spread, and larger than what everyone called the Hacienda. That long, low house didn't have pristine marble floors glistening like mirrors and columns as formal as the ones he'd seen in a casino in Las Vegas when they'd made a delivery out to the desert about six months ago.

A staircase curved up to an open gallery on the second story. On either side of the front door, rooms were two steps below the entry's marble floor. Furniture that looked like it belonged in a mansion was arranged in each. None appeared comfortable.

A plain woman didn't fit in this setting. Neither did he.

"How long," J.J. asked, "will it take us to get to our next stop?"

"From what I saw on the map, I'd guess about three hours."

The two of them took turns driving and keeping track of their route, while Ned rode with the horses. Toby had been on map duty today because J.J. didn't trust a GPS to get them where they needed to go. Many of the farms where they delivered horses were far off the beaten path, making map programs useless.

J.J. frowned for only a second because Sarah reappeared. She carried a tray with a pitcher of lemonade and glasses. Behind her, like ribbons on the tail of a kite, were four youngsters. The oldest had been out on the porch, but there was a little girl and two boys, too. The quartet must be siblings, though the younger two were blond while the older ones had black hair. They couldn't be Sarah's because they wore bright colored shirts and sneakers with soles that lit each time they took a step. Yet, it was clear she was in charge of them.

"If you'll follow me…" Sarah motioned with her head toward her left.

"Let me help you with that big load," Ned said, stepping forward with a grin.

"I'm fine. *Danki*."

"Nonsense. There's no reason for a pretty filly like you to tote such a load." Ned snatched the tray, and lemonade splattered out of the pitcher set in the center.

Dismay skittered across her face, but she turned to the kids, who'd skipped ahead of her into the big room, where they each grabbed a seat, the younger two wanting the same one. She convinced them to share as Ned put the tray on a low table. She turned and bumped into him. Without a word, she edged away.

Toby glanced at J.J. His boss was frowning. Ian Summerhays was an important client, and J.J. wouldn't want Ned's antics to cause problems. The plan when they left the ranch in Texas was for Ned to remain behind for a couple of weeks with the horses delivered to Summerhays. If J.J. changed his mind...

With a frown, Toby walked to a nearby sofa. If J.J. decided he couldn't trust Ned—and he had plenty of reasons not to, assuming half the things Ned bragged about were true—Toby would be stuck at the fancy stables. Not that he wouldn't have liked to spend more time getting the horses he'd worked with acclimated, but he'd hoped to use the time without Ned to ask J.J. about starting a small herd of his own. It would give him deeper roots on the ranch, something he'd never had while living with vagabond parents.

He hoped the rough seams on his denims wouldn't snag the smooth lustrous material on the couch. He made sure his worn boots weren't anywhere near the expensive upholstery or the wood that looked as if it'd been whitewashed. Everything about the house shouted the owners had spent a bundle on it.

They should have worried more about comfort, he thought as he sat. The chairs and sofas seemed too fragile and tiny for a full-grown man. His boss looked as if he perched on nursery furniture, because his knees rose to his chest level.

While Sarah served them lemonade, Ned kept trying

to catch her eye. She stiffened each time he came close, but kept a smile in place as she told the youngsters they could have lemonade in the breakfast room.

Toby guessed she was their nanny. He thanked her when she handed him a glass that was frosted from the humidity, though the air-conditioning was keeping the house cool.

Ned moved too near to her when she offered him a glass. His broad hand closed over the glass and her hand. Her faint gasp brought Toby to his feet.

J.J. didn't stand as he fired a glance at Toby, a warning to sit. At the same time, his boss asked, "Why don't you drink that while you check on the horses, Ned?"

"I—"

"Never hurts to check again."

Ned gave Sarah a broad smile but aimed a scowl at Toby as he strode out of the room.

J.J. motioned for Toby to remain sitting. Toby wasn't sure why. Did Sarah have any idea that Ned was going to be remaining at the farm while Toby and J.J. left to deliver the rest of the horses?

Wishing he had an excuse to leave the ornate room where most of the surfaces seemed to be covered with gold leaf, Toby sipped the tart lemonade. Sarah still appeared uncomfortable, he realized, as J.J. smiled at her.

"May I ask you a personal question, young lady?" he asked.

Toby swallowed a silent moan. He recognized that grin. His boss was about to shake up what he considered a dull discussion. When J.J. looked at him, Toby guessed what his boss was about to ask. If he could think of a way—any way—to distract J.J., he would have. Stopping J.J. was about as easy as halting a charging bull with a piece of tissue paper.

"Of course." Sarah squared her shoulders, preparing herself for whatever J.J. had to say.

"Are you Amish?" J.J. asked.

"I am."

He chuckled and hooked a thumb toward Toby. "Like you. How do you say it, Toby? Like you, ain't so?"

"You're Amish?" A flush rushed up her cheeks, and he could tell Sarah wished the question would disappear.

Toby nodded as he waited for her to ask one of the next obvious questions. The ones he was always asked. If he was Amish, why was he traveling with J.J. and Ned delivering horses? Where did he live when he wasn't on the road? Was he related to—or knew—someone connected to her? He hated the questions as much as he hated the answers he'd devised to skirt the truth.

Almost fifteen years ago, when he'd first gone to work for J.J., he'd answered those questions. He'd explained traveling wasn't new to him. It was the life he'd always known. His parents had moved from one Amish settlement to another, seldom staying longer than six months, sometimes less than a week before heading somewhere new. They'd done that for as long as he could remember. He'd learned not to establish close relationships because soon he'd be leaving them behind. How could he have fun flirting with girls when he'd be going soon, breaking her heart as well as his own?

His life had changed after the family had arrived at a settlement in southern Texas. They'd stayed eight months. Toby had found work he loved: training horses at J.J.'s ranch. When his parents left, he'd stayed. The ranch was perfect for him. People and horses came and went. He didn't have to worry about being the only outsider.

When he'd shared honest answers, he'd gotten pity or, worse, someone wanting to help him. To accept assistance would mean obligations he didn't want. He'd created other answers. Not lies, but not the whole truth, either.

"Ja," he said, letting himself slip into *Deitsch* for a moment.

"If you're here on Sunday, you're welcome at our services," she replied in the same language before turning to J.J. and asking in English if he wanted more lemonade.

Toby was taken aback at her lack of curiosity. Why hadn't she posed the questions others had? Was she worried he'd have questions of his own? Was she hiding something like he was?

He'd never know if he left as soon as the horses were unloaded. Guilt clamped a heated claw around his throat. How could he leave her here with someone like Ned, who would see a plain woman as an easy target for his heartless flirtations? Should Toby suggest J.J. take Ned with him and let Toby stay instead?

You've lost your mind! The best thing he could do was get out of there as soon as possible. He needed to avoid the faintest possibility of a connection with Sarah, a lovely woman who intrigued him. Maybe it was too late. His determination to keep Ned from breaking her heart proved that. He didn't want to see her hurt as he'd been many times.

Chapter Two

Sarah had never been so relieved to see her boss as she was when Mr. Summerhays strode into the room. J.J. had been telling an endless tale about people she'd never met in places she'd never heard of. Her polite interruptions to offer lemonade hadn't stymied him. He would reply that he'd like more to drink; then once again, he'd relaunch into his story. He shared a multitude of events that were, in Sarah's opinion, barely related to one another. When he mentioned Toby by name, she was surprised to hear him say he was glad to have Toby with him because they could share the driving on long trips.

She wondered if J.J. found Ned overly pushy, too. Instantly, she was contrite. She shouldn't judge *Englisch* folks and their ways when she was considering becoming one of them.

"Thank you, Sarah," Mr. Summerhays said with his easy smile as he entered the room. To look at him, nobody would think he was a wealthy man. He dressed in beat-up clothes and always appeared to be in desperate need of a haircut. He was the complete opposite of his wife, who never emerged from their room without makeup, a perfect hairdo and clothing that had graced the pages of the fashion magazines she read.

Sarah nodded and rose. Thanking God for putting an end to the stilted conversation that felt as if every word had to be invented before she could speak it, she left the lemonade and extra glasses on the table.

As she reached the door, she spread out her arms to halt Ethan and Mia from racing in and interrupting their *daed*. She quickly realized they didn't want to see him, but the horses Natalie had told them were in the trailer.

Sarah's heart grew heavy at the thought that the *kinder* weren't interested in spending time with their *daed*, though they hadn't seen him for a week. How she wished she could have another few moments with her *daed*! He'd died before she and her two older brothers had moved to the Harmony Creek settlement. Unlike Menno and Benjamin, *Daed* had listened to her dreams of finding a way to help others. Her brothers dismissed them as silly, but *Daed* never had. When she'd suggested she take EMT training when they became volunteers at the Salem Fire Department, her brothers had reminded her that they were the heads of the household.

And they disapproved of the idea.

As one, they told her she must not mention it again and should focus on more appropriate duties. No Amish woman should be giving medical aid to strangers. It wasn't right.

Neither Benjamin nor Menno was being honest with her. They were worried she'd get hurt if she served as an EMT. Maybe their being overprotective wouldn't have bothered her if Wilbur Eash hadn't been the same. When Wilbur had first paid attention to her at youth group gatherings in Indiana, she'd been flattered such a *gut*-looking and popular guy was interested in her. Before the first time he took her home in his courting buggy, he'd started insisting she heed him on matters big and small. He, like her brothers, seemed to believe she wasn't capable of taking care of herself.

What would *Daed* have said? The same, or would he have suggested she find out if Menno and Benjamin—and Wilbur—were right in their assumption that she needed to be protected from her dreams? *Daed* had always listened to *Mamm's* opinion until her death a few years before his. Sarah had heard him say many times *Mamm's* insight had often made him look at a problem in another way.

She'd asked her friends if they knew of Amish women taking EMT training. They hadn't but offered to write to friends in other settlements. So far, no one had received answers to their letters.

"We'll go ahead and get those horses unloaded," J.J. said from the room behind her. "Toby, tell Ned to help you."

"Can we watch?" Ethan asked as Toby hurried out the front door.

"We'll be good," his little sister hurried to add.

Sarah didn't answer as she pushed her uneasy thoughts aside and concentrated on her job. She loved these *kinder*, but she had no illusions about what rascals they were. Her predecessors hadn't stayed long, according to Mrs. Hancock, because they couldn't handle the rambunctious youngsters. With a laugh, Sarah had replied she'd been quite the outrageous youngster herself, which, she acknowledged, was one reason her brothers looked askance at every idea she had. Though she was twenty-seven, they treated her as if she were as young as Mia. She wished they'd give her the benefit of the doubt once in a while and realize she was a woman who yearned to help others.

Just as she needed to offer the Summerhays *kinder* a chance to show they could be *gut*. Giving the youngsters a stern look, she said, "I'll agree to take you outside to watch if you promise to stay with me every second, hold my hand and not get in the way. If Mr. Christner says you have to leave, you must."

Though the Amish didn't use titles, even when speaking of bishops and ministers, she wanted to impress on the *kinder* how vital it was to heed Toby's instructions while he put the horses in the paddock. Racehorses were high-strung, and she guessed he and Ned needed to keep their attention on the task.

"Can we come, too?" asked Alexander, who was going to be as tall as his *daed* and maybe broader across the shoulders. He was nine, but the top of his head was two inches higher than Sarah's.

She'd never figured out how these *kinder* learned what was going on when she hadn't seen them nearby. She suspected they put the decorative columns and other architectural elements in the house to *gut* use.

"Ja," she said, looking each youngster in the eyes. "You may come, but Ethan and Mia must hold my hands. Natalie, hold Mia's other one. Alexander, hold Ethan's. If anyone lets go, I'll bring you inside right away, and there'll be no going out until the horses are unloaded. Do you agree?"

The *kinder* shot wary glances at each other. When she repeated her question, they nodded.

Sarah took the younger two by the hands and watched to be certain Natalie and Alexander did as she'd requested. Leading them onto the porch, she paused as Toby opened the trailer. She breathed a sigh of relief to see Ned sitting in the truck, going through a stack of paperwork. Tossing it aside, he stepped out of the truck and flashed her a wide smile.

She looked away and right at Toby, who stood with one foot on the bumper. Under his straw hat, a faint frown appeared again as his brows drew together. His eyes were concealed by the shadow from the hat's brim.

Realizing she should have spoken to him before she agreed to bring the *kinder* outside, she asked, "Is it a problem if we watch you unload the horses?"

"Not if you stay out of the way," he answered.

"I'll make sure."

His only reply was an arch of one eloquent eyebrow. She'd heard cowboys could be men of few words, but this one took being terse to ridiculous lengths.

Herding the *kinder* to the far side of the pair of linked paddocks in front of the main stable behind the house, she knew they'd have an excellent view of the proceedings. She'd vetoed Ethan's request to stand on a bench because it was too close to the gate. She wanted the youngsters as far as possible from the animals when they emerged from the trailer and had room to show their displeasure at being transported in close quarters. Sarah was grateful the Texans would be on their way soon. She hadn't expected to have a *gut*-looking Amish cowpoke come into her life.

A faint memory stirred, and she remembered a letter she'd read in *The Budget*, the newspaper printed for and written by scribes in plain communities, about new western settlements that had developed ways that differed from other communities. One in eastern Oklahoma had started using tractors in their fields, because a team of mules couldn't break the soil. The tractors had steel wheels with no tires and couldn't be used for anything but fieldwork, but it was a compromise the settlement had to agree upon if they wanted to remain on those farms.

Toby's settlement in Texas must have made similar concessions to the climate and the land. That could explain why he was allowed to drive the big truck, something that wouldn't have been allowed in most settlements.

The *kinder* began to cheer when Ned brought the first horse and Toby went into the paddock. She hushed them as the big black shied when it came off the ramp. She wasn't sure if her warning or Toby's scowl silenced them. Either way, none of the youngsters made a peep as Ned guided the horse into the first paddock, shoved the reins in Toby's hand and, leaving, closed the gate.

Toby began to give the sleek horse a quick examination. "I need to make sure, while the horse was in the trailer, he didn't injure himself without us noticing," he said, answering the question she'd been thinking but hadn't wanted to ask out loud.

She watched how Toby ran his hands along the horse, keeping it from shying away or rearing in fright. He kept his motions to a minimum, and if the horse began to tense, he soothed it with soft words.

Satisfied the horse was fine, Toby led him into the inner paddock and took off the lead rope. The horse galloped, happy to be out of the trailer and able to stretch out his legs.

"Pretty horse," Natalie said in a wistful tone. The girl was as obsessed with horses as her *daed*.

The second horse, also dark in color, took his arrival in stride. He pranced into the paddock, dragging Ned with him, and stood like a statue during the examination. When Toby turned him out in the other paddock, he walked in as if coming home.

"That was easy," Alexander said with a grin. "Too bad they aren't all like that."

Toby nodded but didn't smile in return. Maybe his lips grew a little less taut.

When Alexander looked at her with an expression that asked *What did I do wrong?* she smiled and said, "Mr. Christner needs to concentrate. I'm sure he'll be more ready to talk once he's done."

She *wasn't* sure of that or why she was making excuses, other than she didn't want Alexander to be hurt. The boy nodded, and she turned as the *kinder* did to watch the final horse being taken from the trailer.

Even she, who didn't know much about horses beyond the quiet buggy horse she drove, could tell the bay prancing around Ned was magnificent. Muscles rippled beneath the sheen of his coat, and his black mane and tail floated on the air with each movement.

As soon as the horse was brought into the first paddock, Toby began the same swift examination he'd done with the others. He was squatting, checking the horse's legs, when a gray barn cat flashed through the paddock. The horse started, whinnied, then reared in a panic.

Sarah tightened her grip on the younger *kinder's* hands and called to Natalie and Alexander to back away from the fence. The horrified youngsters froze as the bay's hooves pawed the air as if fighting off a giant invisible rival.

Mia screamed, "Look out, kitty!"

The little girl tore her hand out of Sarah's and lunged toward the fence. Sarah grabbed Mia by the shoulders, tugging her back as the horse bucked toward them.

"Hold my hand and don't let go," Sarah ordered in not much more than a whisper. She didn't want her voice to upset the horse more, though she doubted it could be heard in the paddock over the thuds from the horse's hooves on the ground. "Nobody move. Nobody say a word."

She stared at the paddock, horrified. Toby tried to calm the horse. He kept the horse from bucking by guiding it away from the fence. The horse jerked forward. He stumbled after it, refusing to let go of the lead. He grimaced and stutter-stepped. Dropping to one knee, he pushed himself up again. Fast.

Not fast enough. The horse was spinning to strike out at him again. It yanked the lead away from him.

Releasing the *kinder's* hands, Sarah pushed aside the gate and ran into the paddock. Toby shouted as the Summerhays kids cried out in fear. Ned called a warning. She ignored them and tried to grab the rope, ducking so it didn't strike her.

She'd handled a frightened animal before. When a new buggy horse had been spooked by a passing truck, she'd known she needed to reassure the horse and show it there was nothing to fear.

Not looking at the horse directly, she kept talking as she evaded its flashing hooves. She was relieved when Toby grabbed the horse's halter. He stroked the shuddering animal but didn't say anything while she continued to murmur. The horse began to grow calmer.

When she thought it was safe, she asked, "Where do you want him?"

"The inner paddock with the others." Toby's voice was clipped.

Was he upset with her for stepping in? No time to ask. She walked the horse to the gate and into the paddock. Unsnapping the lead, she moved slowly to keep from scaring the horse again.

The moment Sarah closed the gate, Alexander called out, "That was cool, Sarah!"

"Quiet. There's no sense upsetting the horses more."

Not waiting to see if the kids would cooperate, she went to where Toby was leaning against a fence post.

"How badly are you hurt?" she asked.

Instead of answering her, he asked, "Is Bay Boy okay?"

"He's shivering," she said, glancing at the other paddock, "but he'll be okay."

"You've got a way with horses."

When she saw how he gritted his teeth on each word, she said, "You are hurt! Where?"

"I twisted my ankle. It'll be okay once I walk it off." He pushed himself away from the rail and took a step to prove it.

With a gasp, he sank to his left knee and grasped his right ankle.

She scanned the yard. Where was Ned? She didn't see him anywhere.

"Alexander," she shouted, "go inside and call 911. Right now!"

"I can call them from here." He pulled a cell phone out of his pocket.

"Quickly!"

Later, she'd remind Alexander he wasn't supposed to have his phone for another week. He'd gotten in trouble while prank calling his friends because he was bored. By mistake, he'd reached the private phone of the police chief in the village of Salem. She wondered how the boy had retrieved his phone. She'd asked Mr. Summerhays to put it in his wall safe. With a grimace, she guessed Alexander had watched his *daed* open it often enough that he'd learned the combination. She'd have to find another way to make him atone for bothering the police chief.

At that thought, she added, "Dial carefully."

He averted his eyes, a sure sign he knew a scolding would be coming his way once Toby was taken care of.

The call was made, and Alexander reported the rescue squad was on its way. He gave her the phone. Dropping it into a pocket under her black apron, she looked at Toby, who was trying not to show his pain.

Just as he hid every other emotion. What was he worried about revealing?

Everything, in Toby's estimation, had gone wrong since J.J. had pulled the truck into the Summerhays' long drive. The moment Toby had gone to the door and found an Amish woman there, he should have known this wasn't going to be like other deliveries they'd made on this trip from Texas. He hadn't guessed he'd be hurt by a horse he'd trained himself. A beginner's mistake. After years of working with horses and convincing them it was better to behave, he should have been prepared for every possible move Bay Boy could have made.

At the worst moment, as the cat decided to chase something right under Bay Boy's nose, Toby had let himself be distracted by Sarah and how the reflected sunlight off her gorgeous red hair seared his eyes. *Dummkopf,* he chided himself. He spent the past dozen years avoiding relationships, romantic or otherwise, and he'd been at Summerhays Stables less than two hours and already was thinking too much about her.

"Ned?" he managed to ask.

Sarah shrugged her slender shoulders. "I don't know where he went. *Komm* with me," she said in a tone that suggested he'd be wasting his time to protest. He guessed she used it often with the Summerhays kids. "You need to get your weight off that ankle before you hurt it worse."

He wasn't sure he could hurt it worse. Each time he took a breath, stabs of pain danced around his ankle, setting every nerve on fire.

"I'm fine right here." The idea of moving was horrifying.

"There's a bench on the other side of the fence. You can sit there until the EMTs arrive."

She didn't give him a chance to protest. Squatting, she moved beneath his right arm, which she draped over her shoulders. The top of her *kapp* just missed his chin. She put her arm around him. With a strength he hadn't expected, she assisted him to his feet. His face must have displayed his surprise.

"I've been wrangling four *kinder*, cowboy," she said in an easy copy of his boss's drawl. "One bumped-up cowboy is easy."

"I'm sure it is." He glanced at where the kids were watching, wide-eyed.

Why hadn't she sent them into the house? He didn't need an audience when he hopped along like a hobbled old man.

Pride is a sin. His *daed's* voice ran through his head. *Daed* had always been skilled at preaching the dangers of *hochmut*. Maybe if he'd been a bit less judgmental, the family could have settled somewhere instead of continuously moving to another district.

Sharp pain coursed up his leg and down to his toes. Had he broken something? He didn't think so. Was it *only* a sprain? Each movement was agonizing.

"It's not far," Sarah said.

To herself or to him? His weight must have been wearing on her slender shoulders, though she didn't make a peep of complaint.

A scent that was sweet and woodsy at the same time drifted from her hair. She was careful to help absorb each motion as she helped him from the paddock and out onto the grass.

"This is far enough," he said, panting as if he'd run across Texas.

"You're right." She hunkered down and let his arm slide off her shoulders.

"I'm sorry if I hurt you."

"I'm okay." She smiled, but her eyes were dim enough to confirm he was right. Her shoulders must be aching.

Toby was grateful when she waved the *kinder* aside and urged them to let him get some air. He thought they'd protest, but they turned as one when the distant sound of a siren resonated off the foothills, rising beyond the stable.

"They're coming!" the older boy—Toby couldn't recall his name through the curtain of pain—shouted.

The siren got louder moments before a square and boxy ambulance appeared around the side of J.J.'s trailer. The kids let out squeals of excitement, but Sarah hushed them. Had she guessed every sound reverberated through his throbbing ankle?

Two men jumped from the ambulance. Each one carried emergency supplies. Shouts came from the direction of the house, and Toby recognized his boss's anxious voice.

What a mess he'd made of this! The boy he'd once been would have offered a prayer to God to bring him fast healing, but he couldn't remember the last time he'd reached out to God. He didn't want to make that connection, either, remembering how his Heavenly Father seemed to stop listening to his prayers when *Daed* had

moved them yet again before Toby had even finished unpacking the two boxes he took with him from one place
to the next.

"Hi, Sarah!" said a dark-complexioned EMT who wore
thick glasses. "What happened here?"

She explained and introduced Toby to the man she
called George. The other EMT, a short balding man, was
named Derek. They worked on the volunteer fire department with her brothers.

He didn't want to know that. Everything she said,
everyone she introduced him to, every moment while
depending on someone threatened to make a connection to the farm and the community beyond it. To say
that would sound ungrateful. He needed to focus on
getting on his feet again so he could help with their
next delivery.

As they knelt beside him, the two EMTs began asking him question after question. *Ja*, he replied, his right
ankle hurt. No, he hadn't heard a cracking sound when
he stepped wrong. *Ja*, he'd stepped on it after feeling
the first pain. No, it didn't radiate pain except when he'd
hopped to where he sat.

"Let's get a look at it," George said with a practiced
smile. "Sorry if this hurts."

That was an understatement. When George shifted
Toby's right foot and began to slip off his boot, the world
telescoped into a black void of anguish sparked with
lightning.

"Stay with us, Toby," crooned Derek as he pushed up
Toby's sleeve and grabbed an IV needle and tube. "Slow
deep breaths. Draw the air in and hold it and let it out.
Nice and slow." He kept repeating the words in a steady
rhythm that was impossible not to follow.

The darkness receded, and the sunshine and the smells of animals and dirt rushed to awaken Toby's senses.

"Back with us?" George asked.

"I think so."

"Good. Breathe deeply. It'll keep you from getting light-headed." The EMT stuck the needle into Toby's left arm.

Though Toby didn't wince, he heard the kids groan in horror.

Sarah hushed them but gasped, "Oh, my!" when George rolled down Toby's sock with care.

Her reaction was a warning, but Toby was shocked to see how swollen his ankle was. Twice its usual size, it was turning as purple as an eggplant.

"What's happening here?" called J.J. as he reached the paddock with Mr. Summerhays in tow. Ned trailed after them like a half-forgotten pup. He must have gone inside to alert their boss to what had happened.

"A horse wanted to dance," Toby replied with grim humor, "but he didn't want me to lead."

"Is he hurt bad?" J.J. looked past him to the EMTs.

"We'll know when we get X-rays at the hospital," George said.

"Hospital?" Toby shook his head. "Bind it, and it'll be fine."

"I didn't realize you were a doctor, Mr. Christner."

The kids giggled on cue, and Sarah smiled at the EMT's jest. Yet, in her gaze, he could see her anxiety. He wanted to tell her not to worry about him, though he guessed he'd be wasting his breath. As much as she focused on the *kinder*, she might be the type to fret about every detail of every day.

The last kind of person he needed in his life.

If that was so, why did he keep thinking about how

sweet it'd been to lean on her? She'd been strong and soft at the same time, a combination that teased him to learn more about her.

Toby shut his mouth before he could say something. Something that would make him embarrass himself more. He'd thought nothing could be worse than the pain in his ankle, but he'd been wrong. The only way to keep from saying the wrong thing again was to do what he always tried to do: say nothing.

Chapter Three

Hushing the *kinder*, Sarah moved aside to let the EMTs stabilize Toby's ankle. How useless she felt! If she'd had the training she yearned for, she could have helped him instead of having to wait for the rescue squad to arrive.

"Sarah?"

She looked at Mr. Summerhays, who crooked a finger to her. Telling the youngsters not to move or interrupt the EMTs, she went to where her boss stood by the paddock fence.

Without preamble, he said, "I want you to go to the hospital with him."

"Me? But why?" The words were out before she could halt them.

"Someone needs to go." He glanced at J.J.

Sarah understood what her boss didn't say. He wanted to get his business with the Texan taken care of as soon as possible. With the racing season underway at Saratoga, Mr. Summerhays made it a practice never to miss a single race of his horses or horses that might compete with his.

"Ned could go," she said.

"Ned?" When she looked past Mr. Summerhays toward the overbearing cowboy, he frowned. "We're going to need an extra hand to get the horses settled."

"The *kinder*… I mean, the children—"

He interrupted her. "Leave them with Mrs. Beebe. She can watch them for the rest of the afternoon."

"Okay." What else could she say? Mr. Summerhays was her boss, and he was the *kinder's daed*.

He held out a cell phone. "Use this to call for a ride when you're done at the hospital."

"I have a phone." She pulled out Alexander's.

"Oh." Mr. Summerhays looked puzzled for a moment, not recognizing his son's cell phone. "Well, good. I trust you to make sure he gets the best possible care. I'll call the hospital to let them know that I'm responsible for the bill."

"*Ja*, sir." Though husband and wife were too distracted with their pursuits to give their *kinder* the time and attention they craved, they were generous. "I'll call you—" She halted herself when he raised a single finger. "I meant, of course, I'll call the house when we're done at the hospital."

"I can go and get him," J.J. said as he came closer.

Mr. Summerhays waved aside his words. "Nonsense. There's no need for you to put yourself out. Sarah can handle it. She's had a lot of practice dealing with small crises like this."

Wondering if Toby would describe his injured ankle as a *small* crisis, Sarah nodded as the two men turned to go to the house. When Mr. Summerhays paused long enough to remind her the *kinder* should be left with Mrs. Beebe, Sarah nodded again. She was sure the cook was going to be annoyed. Mrs. Beebe had to prepare food for the household while the kitchen was being taken apart. She would be relieved when it was redone with the finishes Mrs. Summerhays had chosen before she left for Europe, but the end of the project was still weeks away.

Sarah gathered the *kinder* and led them toward the house, though she would have preferred to stay and watch George and Derek work. Taking the youngsters up the ramp into the kitchen, she wasn't surprised when Mrs. Beebe, who was as thin as one of the columns, frowned.

"Now?" The gray-haired cook sighed as the *kinder* spread out in the huge kitchen, checking the many boxes stacked in every available space, blocking tall windows and cupboards waiting to be ripped out. "If they tip a cabinet on themselves, we'll need another ambulance."

"I'm sorry, but Mr. Summerhays—"

"Go and do what he asked." Mrs. Beebe waved her apron at Sarah. "I'll find something to keep them out of trouble."

Hoping the cook would do better than she had, Sarah rushed outside. She bumped into J.J., who was with Mr. Summerhays.

"Steady there," he said, putting his hands on her shoulders to keep her from falling. "Are you okay? You didn't get hurt, too, did you?"

Assuring him that she was fine, she hurried toward the paddock. She reached it as the two EMTs were raising the gurney with Toby strapped to it. Seeing his straw hat in the dust, she picked it up and carried it toward the ambulance.

Toby's face was in full view without his hat. She was startled to see, in spite of his face's strong lines and angles, a hint of boyishness that had been hidden before. Was pain forcing him to lower his guard a tiny bit?

"I appreciate your retrieving my hat," Toby said, holding out his hand for it. *"Danki."*

She didn't give it to him. "Let's wait until we're in the ambulance."

"We?" He started to sit up.

When Derek cautioned him to remain still, Toby leaned back against the pillow. He glared at her. She hoped he'd understand when she explained her boss— and his—had sent her with him. Maybe then he'd see she wasn't any happier about this situation than he was.

Her prayer from earlier echoed in her mind. *God, grant me patience. Please let this be the last time I have to save these little ones from their antics. At least for today...*

She needed to be more careful what she prayed for.

Toby tested his ankle, shifting it as he sat in a wheel-chair in the emergency waiting room. He couldn't move the thick air-cast boot encasing his leg enough to do more than cause him pain. Had he groaned aloud? A woman stopped and asked if he needed a nurse. Thanking her, he shook his head.

He was glad when she kept going. Each person who passed by, and there were a lot, glanced his way and added to his self-consciousness.

Two hours ago, after a half-hour drive over pothole-ridden roads, he'd arrived at Glens Falls Hospital. Since then, he'd been subjected to X-rays, examinations and questions. He'd started to wonder if every member of the hospital staff had stopped in to see the useless man who couldn't control a horse he'd trained for the past year.

Every member of the hospital staff except a *doktor.*

Finally, a short man had walked in wearing a white lab coat. He'd introduced himself as *Doktor* Garza before saying, "You did a real number on your ankle, Mr. Christner."

The words had stung like a rebuke. He'd let his attention wander, and he was paying the price.

"How long before I can work?" Toby had asked.

"You shouldn't put full weight on it for eight weeks."

"Eight *weeks*?"

Doktor Garza had sighed. "I know it's not what you wanted to hear, but to be honest, I haven't seen anyone sprain an ankle quite that bad in a long time. You're going to need to work with a physical therapist to strengthen the muscles so you don't injure them again. If you don't—"

A laugh from the cubicle where Sarah had gone with a nurse intruded into his thoughts about what *Doktor* Garza had said before leaving to check his next patient.

The desk was right behind where Toby now waited. He hadn't listened to their conversation, but he sat straighter when Sarah spoke.

"Oh, it's no worry," she said with another easy laugh. "I can make sure everything is taken care of. I'm used to dealing with recalcitrant kids, big and small."

The nurse chuckled, but Toby didn't.

Was Sarah referring to him? He wasn't going to be her problem. Once he returned to Summerhays Stables, he'd be on his way. The tenuous connection between him and the pretty redhead would be broken.

After he left there, what would he do?

Eight weeks!

Eight weeks of being unable to assist J.J. If his boss sent him back to Texas, he'd be as useless there. He couldn't ride, not with the inflated boot on his right foot. He couldn't take care of the animals, even the ones in the barns, because shoveling out a stall would be impossible on one leg.

Toby looked up when Sarah came around the side of

the cubicle, carrying a white plastic bag. She gave him a taut smile.

"It'll be at least forty-five minutes before someone can get here," she said, taking a seat next to his wheelchair.

"Have you seen my boot? My regular boot."

She pointed to the white bag on the chair beside her. "It's in here with your instructions and prescriptions you'll need to get filled. Do you want to see?"

"No hurry. It sounds as if I won't be wearing my boot for a few days."

"Are you hungry?" she asked in the gentle tone he'd heard her use with the Summerhays kids.

He couldn't keep from thinking about how she'd told the nurse she was accustomed to taking care of stubborn *kinder*. Had she cast him in that role? "Not really."

"Thirsty?"

He sighed. She was determined to take care of him as if he were a Summerhays youngster. How could he fault her for lumping him in with the rambunctious *kinder*? He'd been rude to her from the first word he'd spoken, and she'd made every effort to be nice. He doubted he could have acted the same if their circumstances were reversed. It was long past time for him to show her a bit of gratitude. She'd ridden in the bumpy ambulance with him and waited two long hours in an uncomfortable chair while he was tended to.

"I'm a bit thirsty," he replied.

"Me, too. There's a snack shop. We've got plenty of time to get something before the car arrives."

When she stood, he almost apologized for his curt replies. She didn't give him a chance as she handed him the plastic bag and grasped the handles of the wheelchair.

Toby grimaced as he caught the plastic bag before it could slide off his lap. He'd thought sitting by the entrance door was the most humiliating thing he could experience, but being pushed along the hallway as if in the middle of a bizarre parade was worse. The scents of disinfectants and floor polish followed them.

Behind him, Sarah kept up a steady monologue. He didn't listen as they turned a corner. The slight jar sent pain surging through him.

When she steered the chair through a door as easily as he would have sent a well-trained horse into its stall, he saw a half-dozen colored tables. A pile of cafeteria trays was stacked to his right, and three people were pushing theirs along rails as they selected food and drinks. A woman with a hairnet and apron assisted them.

"What do you want?" Sarah asked.

"I'll have whatever you're having."

"I was going to have a cup of tea."

His nose wrinkled. "Make mine a cup of *kaffi*. Black."

Sarah left him by an empty table and went to get a tray. Carrying it to the far end of the rails, she spoke to the woman in the hairnet, took two blue cups and went to the cash register.

Realization dawned on him, and when she set a cup of fragrant *kaffi* in front of him, he said, "Before we leave, I need to talk to someone about paying for this."

"This?" She looked from his cup to hers in bafflement.

"No, the bill for the emergency room."

Reaching for a packet of sugar, she sprinkled it into the tea. "Don't worry. Mr. Summerhays is taking care of it."

"No!" He lowered his voice when heads turned toward them. "I mean, I'm grateful, but I pay my bills."

"You'll have to discuss that with Mr. Summerhays." Her voice was unruffled as she stirred her tea and then took a sip.

"I will. I don't like being beholden to anyone."

Sarah laughed as she had while talking with the nurse. "You say that as if I'm supposed to be surprised."

Lowering his gaze to his *kaffi*, Toby said, "Sorry. I know I'm prickly."

"As a blackberry bush."

"Danki." His lips twitched.

"It's okay. It's *gut* to see you can smile. I won't tell anyone and ruin your stern cowboy reputation."

"Stern? Is that what you think I am?" He looked at her in spite of himself.

She was staring into her cup. "I think it's what you want the world to believe you are. Or maybe you were going for forbidding or contrary. They look pretty much the same to me."

"How's that?"

"As if you sat on a porcupine." When she raised her eyes, they were twinkling with amusement.

"No, you can be certain that if I'd sat on a porcupine, folks would have heard me yelp from here to the Rio Grande." He wasn't sure if he should blame the pain arcing across his ankle or the drugs he'd been given to ease it for giving her such a playful retort.

When she laughed, her eyes widened when he didn't join in.

"Sorry," she said. "I know you're feeling lousy."

Seizing the excuse she'd offered him, he nodded.

They sipped in silence for several minutes. He was amazed the quiet didn't seem to bother her as it had in that fancy room in the Summerhays house. She watched visitors and medical staff coming in and out. An odd expression darkened her eyes when a pair of EMTs wandered in to grab cups of *kaffi*. He thought about asking her if she knew the man and woman, but he kept his curiosity to himself.

Every question he asked, every answer she gave would add a layer to that connection he wanted to avoid.

"Finished?" she asked, coming to her feet.

He was surprised to see his cup was empty. He didn't recall drinking the *kaffi*. His mind wasn't working well.

She took the cup and threw it and her own into a trash can. Coming back, she reached to unlock the chair's brakes.

For a split second, he wondered when she'd set them in place. The sweet aroma of her shampoo drifted to him, and he was tossed back to the moment when she'd helped him in the paddock. Having her holding him close had been enough for him to forget how much his foot hurt. The memory swept over him, diminishing the pain faster than any drug could.

Had he lost his mind? Thinking such things threatened his promise never to get close to anyone again. He needed to be careful. He had to remember how his heart had hurt each time he'd had to leave *gut* friends behind, knowing he'd never see them again. To be honest, somewhere along the way, he'd lost the key to his padlocked heart. He told himself it was for the best. How did he know he wouldn't start acting like his parents, leaving without looking back?

Sarah straightened. "Are you okay? Maybe you should take another pain tablet so it's working by the time the car gets here."

"I'm fine."

"Gut." She bowed her head for a moment.

He thought her prayer would be silent, but she whispered, "God, *danki* for making sure Toby wasn't hurt worse. Please send him quick healing. You know his heart far better than I do, but I don't think he's a patient man."

Gnawing on his bottom lip, he remained silent. He pre-

tended not to see her questioning glance in his direction.
He didn't want to explain he and God had an arrangement
that had worked most of his life. Toby wouldn't expect
anything of God, and God wouldn't expect anything of
him. Knowing that had eased Toby's sorrow each time
his parents decided to move.

That was why a faint twinge deep in his heart as-
tounded him. A twinge of longing? For what? To be close
to God, who had given Toby a life of chaos and loss? He
couldn't see a reason to reach out to his Heavenly Father.
He'd learned to get by on his own.

"Would you like to pray with me?" Sarah asked.

"Not right now. We need to hurry. I don't want to delay
J.J. more than I already have."

She sat facing him again. "Don't you remember? He's
left."

"What?" This time he didn't care that his raised voice
caught the attention of everyone in the snack room. "How
do you know that?"

"I found out when I called for our ride home."

"When were you planning to tell me that little tidbit?"

"I told you while I was wheeling you here."

He started to argue that she hadn't, then recalled how
pain had stripped his mind of everything. She had to be
wrong. J.J. wouldn't go without him.

When he said as much, she shook her head. "I asked
for confirmation when I called, and I was told to tell you
that he and Ned would—"

"Ned left, too? Who's going to help get the horses
settled?"

She shrugged. "I don't know. That's all your boss said.
They'll return in a couple of months to get you."

"A couple of months?" He closed his eyes as waves
of pain flooded him, waves he'd tried to ignore. Open-

ing his eyes, he met Sarah's. "What am I supposed to do until then?"

"Heal."

"Where?"

"I told you. Mr. Summerhays has taken care of everything. There's a guest room on the first floor near the kitchen. You can recover there."

He forced his frustration down. If he'd been thinking straight, he would have known J.J. couldn't stay while Toby went to the hospital. Their schedule was tight, and delaying one place meant upsetting many valuable customers they hoped would give them more work.

Was *this* the answer to his problem on how to protect Sarah from Ned's machinations? He hadn't guessed it'd be for him to have a sprained ankle and be as helpless as a *boppli*.

"I guess I don't have another choice." His voice sounded childish even to his ears. "I'm sorry, Sarah. I—"

"Never mind. We need to be out front for when the car gets here, so let's go," she said with something that sounded like disappointment.

Disappointment? With him?

If so, she would have to get used to that during the next eight weeks. He'd disappointed everyone in his life.

Including himself.

Chapter Four

The second annual Salem Volunteer Fire Department Berry-fest Dinner was well underway by the time Sarah arrived at the new fire station. Parked out front were the big fire engines and the ambulance that had taken Toby to the hospital earlier that day.

That day? To Sarah, it seemed impossible only a few hours had passed since Natalie had come to alert her that a cowboy was on the porch.

After a quiet drive home from the hospital in Mr. Summerhays's luxurious truck, Sarah had been relieved when, as they came into the house, her boss had offered to help get Toby, who was reeling from his pain medication, into the guest room on the main floor. She'd agreed to come early the next day so Mr. Summerhays could finish work he'd had to ignore that afternoon. When he asked her to arrange for Toby's physical therapist's first visit, she realized her boss had added the Texan to her list of responsibilities.

She looked forward to talking with a trained physical therapist, but she wasn't sure how Toby would feel about her involvement.

As she opened the door into the firehouse, she pushed

that concern aside. She was attending the festive dinner with her friends, and she didn't want her mind mired in thoughts of the injured man.

Inside the new fire station, which had been dedicated the previous year, tables were set end to end in three rows. Folding chairs were occupied by neighbors who were enjoying barbecued chicken and salads before the volunteer firefighters served them generous slabs of berry pie. A kitchen could be seen beyond a wide pass-through window where urns held *kaffi* and rows of cups of lemonade and iced tea waited to be claimed. Faint strains of country music came from a speaker in one corner, but it was drowned out by the dozens of conversations in the open space.

A few months ago, heads would have turned when Sarah and her three best friends walked in. However, the residents of the small village had become accustomed to their new plain neighbors among them.

She wondered what the reaction would be if they learned Sarah's friends had jokingly named themselves the Harmony Creek Spinsters' Club. They were too old to belong to a youth group but weren't married, so they didn't fit in anywhere except with each other. As a group, they enjoyed shopping in the village or attending events like the Berry-fest Dinner.

"Where do you want to sit?" asked Annie Wagler, the more talkative of the Wagler twins. She and her sister, Leanna, were at least two inches shorter than Sarah. Their lustrous black hair glowed with a bluish sheen in the station's bright lights.

"Do you see four chairs together?" Sarah scanned the room, seeing many familiar faces. People she'd met in the village as well as those living in the new settlement along Harmony Creek.

"There." Miriam Hartz, a tall blonde, pointed to the right. "Two empty chairs facing two empty chairs."

"Perfect." Sarah led the way. When she sat facing the twins, she smiled as Miriam took the chair next to her.

She was delighted. She hadn't had a chance to talk to Miriam in the past couple of weeks because her friend was busy making preparations for the new school year, which would begin at the end of August. As the Amish school opened two weeks before the private school the Summerhays *kinder* went to, she was hoping to arrange for a visit. Her charges had so many questions about their plain neighbors, and it would be a *gut* way to introduce them to *kinder* their own ages.

"What a *wunderbaar* idea!" Miriam exclaimed when Sarah brought up the subject. "It'll help my scholars, too, by letting them meet younger *Englisch* neighbors. For the most part, their interactions have been with *Englisch* who work in the stores in Salem."

"When do you start school?"

"The last full week of this month."

"The same week as the Washington County fair?"

Miriam gave her a wry smile. "It was either that, or we'd be in session when it was time for next spring's planting. However, we'll be doing half days at the end of the first week, so the scholars and their families can go to the fair later in the day. The days count toward our total, and to be honest, the kids have too much summer on their minds to get much work done."

"Especially as they had to make up days in June and July."

With the disruption of moving into the new settlement in Harmony Creek Hollow, many of the school-age *kinder* hadn't attended the minimum number of days required by the state, so a short session had been necessary. Miriam had held school in her home until the new building had been completed after the Fourth of July.

"I'm hoping they'll be eager to get back to work," Miriam replied, "instead of thinking about playing ball. Some would be happy to do that all day, every day."

The Summerhays kids didn't play ball other than in video games. A basketball court behind the house hadn't been used except for storage of supplies for the house renovation. Other than Natalie, who took every opportunity to be with the horses, the *kinder* preferred to stay indoors. Each time Sarah had insisted on them joining her for a walk, they complained as if being sent to the North Pole in the middle of winter, instead of enjoying the chance to pick fresh berries from the bushes along the road and edging the farm's fields.

"Sarah!"

She stiffened at her older brother's voice, which seemed to silence everyone else. She wondered if Menno's hearing was being damaged by their sawmill. He usually had sawdust clinging to his hair, but tonight it was neat.

Her brothers stopped by where she sat. Menno was short, only an inch or two taller than Sarah. Benjamin's head reached several inches higher than their older brother's. Both were built wide and thick like the stumps they left behind when they felled trees on the wood lot. Benjamin worked at the sawmill, but he'd spent most of his time for the past month planting apple trees.

"Why didn't you tell us you were coming tonight?" asked Menno. "You could have come with us. I don't like the idea of you driving alone after dark."

Heat rose along Sarah's cheeks as eyes turned toward them. Why did her older brother, who was ten years older than she was, treat her as if she were Mia's age? Her brothers had always been protective of her, but since their move to the new settlement, they didn't seem to believe she could breathe without supervision.

"I came with my friends," she said, irritated that her brother's sharp voice had drawn attention to them. "We hired Hank Puente to bring us in his van." She couldn't keep from raising her chin in defiance. "I mentioned that to you at least twice in the past week."

Benjamin nodded with an apologetic smile, but Menno didn't crack his stern facade. For a long moment, her older brother stared at her. She met his gaze, refusing to let him daunt her. At last, he clapped Benjamin on the shoulder and walked away.

"Whew," Annie breathed. "Is it my imagination, or are your brothers keeping an eye on you more closely every day?"

"It's not your imagination."

Leanna reached across the table and patted Sarah's hand in silent consolation.

"That's ridiculous," Miriam said at the same time. "You're a grown woman, not a *boppli*."

With a smile she hoped conveyed her appreciation for her friends coming to her defense, Sarah said, "I've tried to tell them that, but they don't want to listen."

"But they're okay with you working for the Summer-hays family?" Annie asked.

"They haven't said otherwise." She didn't add her brothers knew—as she did—how important her wages were while they worked to establish their sawmill as a viable business.

In the past few weeks, Benjamin and Menno had been discussing the pine trees in their steep fields. A Christmas tree farm is what Benjamin called it, and she guessed that they hoped to sell fresh trees as the holidays approached. Plain families wouldn't buy them, but

Englischers might. However, until the harvest was in and the holiday season rolled around, the household depended on what she was paid each week. That her pay from Mr. Summerhays was always on time was a blessing she never took for granted.

"*Guten owed*, ladies," came a deep voice, silencing her thoughts.

A look over her shoulder wasn't necessary when Sarah saw the soft smile blossoming on Miriam's face. Even if Sarah hadn't recognized the voice as Eli Troyer's, her friend's expression announced how happy Miriam was to see the carpenter who lived at the far end of the hollow. The two had been walking out together for the past few weeks, a fact Sarah had guessed, though neither Miriam nor Eli had said a word.

Setting plates in front of them with a flourish worthy of the finest restaurant, Eli reminded them the dinner was all-you-can-eat.

Sarah chuckled when she looked at her plate heaped with chicken, french fries, and potato, macaroni and green salads. "I can't eat all this."

"Not if we want pie," added Annie with a laugh.

"You definitely want pie." Eli motioned toward the counter. "Help yourself to something to drink, too." He hurried away to serve more food.

"Miriam, how did you arrange for Eli to be our waiter?" Sarah asked with a wink to her friends.

Miriam's face grew as red as the filling in the slices of berry pie arranged on a nearby table, then she smiled. "I didn't, but I'm grateful for small favors."

"I wish more of those handsome firefighters would stop by," said Leanna.

Sarah put her arm around her friend as they went to get their choice of drinks from the counter. She didn't know what to say to Leanna, who was eager to get married since the man she'd fallen for wed someone else.

When she saw how Miriam glowed as Eli spoke to her, Sarah was sure this fall would be Miriam's last as a schoolteacher. Would she marry Eli before Christmas? Though such matters were kept quiet, the small size of the community settled along Harmony Creek made it impossible not to notice who was spending time together.

She wished Miriam every happiness, because Eli seemed like a *gut* man. She prayed the Wagler twins would find such *wunderbaar* matches, too. As for herself, she needed to sort out her future before she could commit the rest of her life to someone. She must not make the same mistake she had when opening her heart to Wilbur Eash and having him assume he could make every decision for her.

"So what trouble did your *kinder* get into today?" Annie asked after they'd shared a silent prayer of thanks for the food in front of them.

Sarah was relieved by Annie's question, which gave her an excuse to shove aside her uncomfortable thoughts. "The high point was when I had to get them off those tall columns in the entry." She stabbed a piece of green salad. "I don't know how you deal with a dozen, Miriam, when I'm on my toes with four."

"The *kinder* didn't get hurt, ain't so?" asked Miriam.

"No." She explained how she'd gotten to the two younger ones before they fell.

"I'm glad to hear that after Caleb mentioned the ambulance went out to the stables this afternoon."

Sarah nodded. Like her brothers, Miriam's brother, who was the founder of the new settlement along Harmony Creek, was a volunteer firefighter. They wore beepers to alert them about emergencies.

"Is everyone okay?" asked Leanna.

Again, Sarah nodded. "Horses were being delivered, and one was startled by a barn cat. When Toby tried to control it, he got hurt. We were worried his ankle was broken, which was why I had Alexander call 911."

"Toby? I think you may have mentioned the name before." Annie glanced at the others as she arched her brows.

Sarah ignored her teasing. "He delivered the three horses to Mr. Summerhays from Texas."

"A cowboy?" Annie asked with a chuckle.

Again Sarah acted as if she hadn't heard the silly question. "Toby was examining the horse when it spooked. He needed to go to the emergency room, but he's at the house now. He'll stay there while his sprain heals." She shook her head. "I'm not sure who's going to give me more trouble, the *kinder* or Toby."

"You'll be taking care of him?" Miriam asked.

"Mr. Summerhays wants me to oversee his physical therapy." She took a bite of the delicious macaroni salad, which tasted like the one served at the last church Sunday. She guessed an Amish volunteer had shared the recipe with the other firefighters. "It was such a bizarre accident. Watching Toby, it's obvious he's skilled with handling horses. If he hadn't been, Mr. Summerhays would have insisted on his grooms checking the horses. It's too bad he was hurt."

Expecting her friends to show sympathy for Toby's situation, Sarah was astonished when the others began laughing.

"What's funny?" she asked.

"You and your Amish cowboy." Annie put her hand to her lips as she giggled again.

"He's not *my* cowboy."

"Not yet."

Turning to Leanna, Sarah said, "Maybe you can talk sense into your twin. She's not listening to me."

"Annie doesn't listen to anyone." With a warm smile for her sister, Leanna added, "This time I've got to agree with her. You seem pretty taken with this cowboy. You've known him for a few hours, and you've talked more about him this evening than anything else."

"I—"

"Don't deny it, Sarah!" Annie winked at her twin and Miriam. "Isn't it true?"

Sarah waited while they laughed again, then, smiling, asked her friends about what they were busy with. Miriam had school plans, and Leanna had recently purchased some goats and hoped to sell their milk and homemade soap at the farmers market in the center of the village.

When the topic didn't shift again to Toby, she was grateful. It wasn't easy to keep the man out of her thoughts. Several times, she found her mind wandering to him and had to focus on the conversation. It'd been a stressful day, and she was thankful God had put her in a place where she'd been able to help.

Eli came to the table, and Sarah was surprised to see she'd eaten the rest of her meal without tasting a bite, including the pie. Hearing the others commenting on how *wunderbaar* the dessert had been, Sarah wished she'd taken notice of it.

She felt a pang of something she didn't want to examine when she saw how Eli smiled at Miriam at the same time his young nephew gave her a hug. She was happy the three were becoming a family. Why the pang? Maybe she was more like Leanna than she wanted to admit. No, that was silly. Sarah didn't need another man telling her what to do in an unnecessary attempt to shield her from her own choices.

In spite of herself, her eyes cut to where her brothers waited to deliver food to the tables. Her brothers laughed and chatted with plain and *Englisch* firefighters. She frowned when she saw Benjamin say something to two women in T-shirts and jeans that were identical to what the other *Englischer* volunteers wore. He seemed okay with those women being firefighters, but he had agreed with Menno that Sarah must not take EMT training.

There must be something she could do to persuade them she deserved the same respect.

God, please help me discover what.

"Is he *ever* going to wake up?" asked one young voice.

Another answered, "Don't know."

"If he doesn't, how are we going to find out if he's a real cowboy?"

"Don't know."

Toby realized the childish voices weren't part of the dream—no, the nightmare—holding him in its grip. Pushing his way out of a collage of disconnected images, he paid no attention to the conversation. How thin were the walls of the motel J.J. had found for them?

Opening his eyes, he realized he wasn't in a rented room. Instead of a pair of beds with worn headboards and a TV set on a narrow chest, Toby stared at a white-and-gold canopy. Wide dark slats supported it, and more of the fancy fabric was draped around each post supporting the top. Sunlight streamed across floors that glistened as if lit from within. On the other side of the bed was...

He shifted to look in the opposite direction. Pain slashed across his ankle and exploded in his head. A groan escaped his clamped lips.

"Is he dying?" asked the first childlike voice.

"Don't know."

"Should we get Sarah?"

Before the second voice could repeat the same words, Toby raised his head. More agony pierced him, but he gritted his teeth and stared along the bed.

Two small forms were silhouetted against the light. Sunshine glistened off their pale hair.

The younger Summerhays kids! What were they doing sitting on his bed? He must be dreaming.

He shifted. More excruciating pain. No, he wasn't asleep.

"Why are you here?" he asked in a raspy voice he didn't recognize.

"Are you a real cowboy?" asked the little boy. "Where's your six-shooter?"

"I don't carry a gun."

"How do you fight off train robbers and cattle rustlers?"

What were the kids' names? Maybe he could remember if his head didn't pound like a sprinter's pulse. "I don't work with cattle. I train horses."

"How about horse rustlers?" asked the little boy.

"No!" cried the little girl. "Don't say that!"

Toby winced at her shrill voice. He was about to ask her to whisper, but the two youngsters began to argue. Each word was a separate blow against his skull.

The door opened, letting in more light and revealing that the *kinder* were dressed in pajamas with cartoon characters flitting across them.

Risking more pain—and getting it—Toby turned his head again. His breath caught when he realized who stood in the doorway, holding a tray.

Sunlight was filtered by Sarah's *kapp* but shone on her

red hair. It accented the curves of her high cheekbones and the outline of her lips that were drawn in a frown. Her brown eyes were focused on her two younger charges.

"Shoo." Her voice was soft enough not to resonate across his aching head, and she put the tray on a white chest of drawers without making a sound.

"You told us that we could talk to him," protested the little boy.

Why couldn't he remember their names? He was sure he'd heard them…was it only yesterday?

"Ethan, you know I meant *after* Toby was awake. After he had his breakfast."

Ethan… That was the little boy's name. What was the girl's?

As if he'd asked aloud, Sarah said, "Mia, you need to put your breakfast dishes in the dishwasher."

The *kind* pouted. "But Mrs. Beebe—"

"Has her chores to do. Putting away your dishes is *your* chore."

When Sarah lifted the youngsters, first one and then the other, off his bed, the slight motion exacerbated the invisible feet marching across his skull. He was grateful she hadn't had them clamber down, which would have made the mattress shake more.

He kept his eyes closed as the sounds of the *kinder* leaving the room ricocheted through his head. A single set of footfalls, so light he guessed Sarah was walking on tiptoe, came across the room. He heard a faint scrape as she picked up the tray and brought it toward the bed.

"Do you need help to sit?" she asked.

He imagined her slender arm sliding beneath him and her warm breath caressing his cheek as it had when she helped him in the paddock. Another groan slipped past his lips.

Distress entered her voice. "Are you okay?"

"I've been better." Putting his hands against the firm mattress, he pushed himself up to lean against the headboard.

"Your meds are here with your breakfast."

"I don't need—"

"The *doktor* insisted you take them for at least three days."

He met her eyes, half expecting her to look away. She didn't as she leaned forward to put the tray on its short legs on either side of his lap. When she straightened, she held his gaze.

"Okay," he said, knowing he was being foolish. She wanted to help him get better.

That was all he should be thinking about. Getting well and getting to work. Spending time with pretty Sarah risked messing with his mind and his plans. He couldn't start thinking, as he had last night before he fell asleep, how it would be interesting to get to know her better.

"I'm sorry Ethan and Mia disturbed you. I told them not to come in until after you'd had breakfast, but I guess they thought I'd said after *they* had breakfast."

"Or their curiosity wouldn't let them wait."

"Curiosity? About what?"

He looked at the tray she'd brought. It held enough food for half a bunkhouse. "They want to know if I'm a real cowboy."

"I'm sure you set them straight."

"I didn't have time. You came to my rescue." He reached for the bowl of oatmeal.

"I'll speak with them again."

"*Gut.* The *doktor* told me to rest for a few days. I'd appreciate it if you kept the kids away."

Her shoulders became more rigid. "I'll do my best."

"From what I saw when we were unloading the horses, they don't listen to you."

"Are you saying it's the *kinder's* fault you're hurt?"

"No, of course I don't blame them for what happened."

"But you blame someone. Me?"

"No, that's not what I meant, either."

"Then what *do* you mean?"

He faltered. He couldn't be honest with her about his concerns of having Ned hanging around and bothering her. In addition, the fact that Toby had allowed himself to be distracted by Sarah was on his shoulders, not hers.

When he didn't answer, she said in a crisp tone, "You should rest while you can." She walked to the door. "Your physical therapist will be here later."

"Sarah?" he called.

Either she didn't hear him or she didn't want to let the conversation continue, because she kept walking. The door closed behind her, leaving him alone with his breakfast, his swollen ankle and the wish he could go back to sleep so he could start the day again.

Chapter Five

The middle-aged man who arrived at the Summerhays house an hour later introduced himself as Howard Abbott when he walked into Toby's room after the briefest knock. He looked as fit as any man working in the saddle at J.J.'s ranch but was dressed in khaki shorts and a black T-shirt. His sneakers were orange with bright yellow swirls and green soles. He carried a box that was big enough to fit Mia in and have room left. As he set it on the floor, Toby heard a clang, though the man had carried it as if it were empty.

"I'm here to do the physical therapy ordered by your doctor," Howard said with a practiced smile that hinted most of his clients weren't pleased to see him.

Toby was. The sooner he could get on his feet, the sooner he could finish training the three horses and find a way to meet J.J. and Ned. No doubt with a plain community nearby, there were *Englischers* who drove Amish to distant places. He'd hire one. He'd already spent too much time at Summerhays Stables.

And with Sarah Kuhns.

He should be grateful Mr. Summerhays was paying for his medical care and for Sarah making sure he was

fed, but gratitude meant connections to others. Those obligations he had to avoid. He'd been miserable amid his
parents' drama, so he knew getting close to people might
seem like a *gut* idea, but it led to misery. The years since
he'd gone to work on J.J.'s ranch had been the calmest
of his life. His time at the Summerhays house would be
brief, and he didn't want to have regrets tugging at his
heart when he left.

"So tell me what happened," Howard said as he moved
elegant fragile-looking chairs aside to open a space on
the fancy gold, white and dark red rug. With a flick of
his wrist, he spread a bright blue mat into place before
setting a single chair on it.

Toby gave him an abridged explanation. When the
physical therapist nodded at various times, Toby guessed
Howard had gone through his hospital records. Howard pulled a computer pad out of his big bag and made
notes while he asked questions about the level of Toby's
pain, when he'd last taken pain medication and where
his ankle hurt most.

The door opened as Toby was pointing to the top of
his right ankle.

Sarah stepped in. "Howard, I'm sorry I'm late." She
pushed a vagrant red-gold strand beneath her *kapp*.

Howard laughed. "Mia or Ethan?"

"Mia this time." Sarah chuckled, her whole face glow-
ing as stress fell away. "She claims as long as she keeps
one hand on the top rail, she's still on the fence and not
in the corral."

The physical therapist shook his head with another
laugh. "I don't know how you keep up with those kids."

"I don't. That's why I'm late. Have you begun?"

Toby noticed how careful she was not to glance in
his direction. He needed to apologize for what he'd said

earlier. Or what he hadn't said. Not that it mattered, because, despite his denials, he'd given her the impression he blamed her for his accident.

He didn't, and he had to persuade her of that. He didn't want to leave unpaid obligations behind him, and he owed Sarah a huge debt for helping him.

"We're just getting started," Howard said before putting the tablet back in his bag. "Let's get to work. First thing, Toby, is to get you up, so swing your legs over the side of the bed." He chuckled. "This will be easier if we don't have 'help' from the kids."

"You know them?" Toby asked as he pushed himself to the edge of the bed. He wanted their attention on his question instead of him.

"Too well." Howard drew the chair closer to the bed and motioned toward it. "I worked with both boys and Natalie about a year and a half ago. Two broken wrists and a broken leg when they discovered they couldn't fly. Mia was the only one who didn't break something, though she got pretty badly bruised. I don't think they'll try again." He glanced toward Sarah. "You weren't here then, were you?"

"No, that was three nannies before me."

"They tried to fly?" Toby asked, raising his arms as Howard put a wide elastic band around Toby's back.

With an ease Toby envied, the physical therapist used the strap as a way to balance them as he drew Toby up onto his left leg. The motion, though he didn't do much to help, left him light-headed.

"Breathe slowly," Howard said. "You've been sitting a long time, so you've got to get used to standing again. The pain meds can make you dizzy, too."

"I didn't take one this morning."

The physical therapist frowned as he lowered Toby

back to the bed. "You need to take them as the doctor told you for at least three days. If the pain gets ahead of you, it's harder to get it under control again. Don't try to muscle through it. Sarah?"

She stepped forward with the pain pills and a glass of water. Howard lowered Toby to the bed, then stepped aside to let her hand Toby the pills and the glass.

He tried to catch her eyes, but she edged away. Swallowing the pills with a hearty gulp of water, he sighed when Howard stepped forward to take the glass. Sarah wasn't going to make it easy for him to apologize.

Again, Howard helped him stand. When Toby swayed, the physical therapist said, "Breathe in and out, deep and slow. In through your nose, out through your mouth."

Toby listened to Howard's calm voice and followed his instructions. The darkness nibbling at the corner of his vision eased and the room no longer threatened to telescope into nothing. Leaning on the other man's shoulder, he hopped to the chair on the mat.

The urge to thank God for Howard's help surprised him. He hadn't felt that impulse in years. Glancing at where Sarah was setting the glass on a table, he wondered if hearing her heartfelt prayers had gotten him thinking about how long it'd been since he'd reached out to God.

No, that was another connection he didn't want to make.

Toby worked on the exercises Howard had given him as the physical therapist talked with Sarah. Toby didn't expect the motions to be so simple or so painful. A roller he needed to move with his foot made his whole right leg ache as if he'd worked for hours. He concentrated on doing the task, barely listening to Howard answer Sarah's questions about why he'd decided on that exercise and what its purpose was. They spoke with medical jargon he couldn't understand. He was astonished Sarah—as a plain woman—was familiar with the words.

He stopped paying attention to them after Howard asked him to pretend to write the letters of the alphabet with his toes. It was agonizing. His ankle spasmed, and he halted the motion as Howard had told him to do if the pain got worse.

"Sarah, will you please hold his shoulders to keep him from looking at his foot?" asked the physical therapist. "I don't want him to get out of alignment in an attempt to do this exercise."

She moved to stand behind the chair. When her fingers settled on his shoulders, he fought not to react. He didn't want her to think he was flinching because he found her touch bothersome. The light brush of her fingertips sent something more powerful—and more pleasurable—than the pain from his ankle coursing through him.

When Howard told Toby to begin again and start "drawing" the letters, the physical therapist was interrupted by a ringing cell phone. He glanced at it, then excused himself.

Just the opportunity Toby had been waiting for. As soon as the other man stepped out of the room, Toby looked at Sarah. "I need to tell you I'm sorry."

"Now isn't the time for anything but going through these exercises," she said in a crisp tone that contrasted with the easy *gut* humor she'd shown Howard.

"I can apologize at the same time."

"You don't have anything to apologize for."

"No?"

"Not to me."

He frowned with pain as the movement tugged at the abused muscles along his ankle. He was about to retort when Howard returned.

"You're all the way to *Q*, I see," the physical therapist said. "Well done, Toby, but you can stop. We don't want to overstrain your ankle. Do the exercises again this afternoon." He looked past Toby. "Sarah, will you be here to help?"

"Ja."

Toby couldn't tell what she was feeling because there was no overt emotion in the single word.

"Good," Howard said. "Any questions before we get you back in bed, Toby?"

"How soon can I go outdoors?" The words burst from him before he had a chance to think.

Before Howard had arrived, Toby had been staring out the window, wishing he was working with Bay Boy and the other two horses, Dominion and Lou. He wanted to be certain they were being properly exercised, because he didn't want to have to start their specialized training from the beginning again. It would add weeks to the process.

"Outdoors?" Howard seemed surprised by the question. He paused, rubbing his chin. "You sprained your ankle yesterday, right?"

Toby nodded. He didn't want to chance his voice revealing how much pain he was in.

"You can go anywhere," the physical therapist said, "as long as you have someone with you. Have you used crutches before?"

Again, he nodded. "I broke a couple of toes a few years ago, and I had to be on them for about three weeks."

"You'll be on them longer this time, but you'll be done with them sooner if you do your exercises."

"Sarah will make sure I do them." Toby wasn't sure if he or Sarah was more shocked at his comment. Just because Howard had asked her to check on him didn't mean she'd be responsible for his physical therapy every day.

His shoulders stiffened, and she drew her hands away. As before, he couldn't guess what she was thinking without turning around and looking.

Howard chuckled. "Sounds like you've been volunteered, Sarah."

"Mr. Summerhays asked me to help him."

"Okay, so I'll need to go over a few things with you. However, first…"

Reversing the process of getting him out of bed, Howard steered Toby onto it.

"I don't want you on crutches for more than a few minutes at a time until you're accustomed to them again," the physical therapist ordered. "A single misstep could do more damage to your ankle. You've twisted it badly. An additional injury could cause permanent harm."

"I get that."

"Then I hope you also understand you're going to have to baby your ankle except when you're doing your exercises. It needs time to heal. If you don't give it time, it's going to make you sorry." A smile eased his grim expression. "That's not a threat, by the way. It's a fact."

"I know."

He didn't have time to say more before Howard gathered his equipment and, with Sarah, left the room.

Toby's fingers curled into fists of frustration on the bed. He had been in this bedroom for a single day and already it felt like a pretty prison as everyone could come and go…except him. He leaned his head against the pillows propped behind him and glared at the ceiling. Never had he imagined eight weeks could feel like an eternity.

"I appreciate your help and the attention you paid today," Howard said while Sarah walked with him to the front door.

"I appreciate you answering my questions."

"Glad to explain. Most people don't care about the details as long as they know they're going to get better. I want you to know I wasn't asking you to help Toby with his physical therapy. Just to remind him in case his meds make him forget. The wheelchair Mr. Summerhays ordered is on the porch. You've had your hands full before, but now…"

He didn't finish.

He didn't have to.

Sarah understood what he meant. She was responsible for Toby's physical therapy in addition to taking care of four boisterous *kinder*. What would Mr. Summerhays have said if she'd told him she couldn't take on another task? Mrs. Hancock, the housekeeper, hadn't been pleased having to agree to take an hour away from her regular duties twice each day to keep track of the youngsters so Sarah could help Toby. If Mr. Summerhays had asked the housekeeper instead…

He wouldn't have done that. Her boss had interviewed Sarah extensively before she was hired. He'd quizzed her about health care and first aid. She'd assumed he'd been interested about the *kinder's* safety, but he must have remembered her enthusiastic responses. That was the sole reason she could imagine for why he'd put her in charge of making sure Toby improved. As with everything her boss did, it was a simple solution…for him.

"You'd make a good physical therapist because you're gentle but steady with the patient." Howard pulled a business card out of his case and held it out to her. "Here's the admissions office information for the school I attended."

She shook her head. "*Danki*, but it isn't our way to go to college."

"Where did you learn enough to ask those questions, then?"

"Reading books."

He arched a graying brow. "I'm impressed, Sarah."

"Learning is simple when it's a subject that interests me." She smiled, wanting to put him at ease again. To halt herself before she blurted out her dream of becoming an EMT, she went on, "Don't ask me about long division."

"No worries. I hated that myself, though I find that I'm using it more often than I'd guessed when it comes to computing various stresses for my patients."

She gave an emoted groan, and he chuckled.

Telling her he'd be back tomorrow afternoon, he left. She didn't even have a moment to savor the idea of taking classes to learn more about medical care.

An angry shriek came from upstairs, and she took the steps two at a time. She couldn't imagine what the *kinder* might be doing now, but she guessed she needed to put a halt to it right away.

Sarah knocked on Toby's door as she balanced the tray Mrs. Beebe had made for his lunch. She took the muffled answer as an invitation to enter.

Opening the door, she faltered as she was about to enter. Toby must have fallen asleep after his exertions, because his sun-streaked hair was tousled and his eyes were now barely open. Gone, for a moment, was the aloof man who seemed to care more about horses than people. Was that an honest expression of gratitude on his face, a hint at the real man he hid behind curt comments and cool stares?

His face hardened. The gentler man, the one who wouldn't be looking for someone to fault for what had happened to him, had vanished.

"Hungry?" she asked in a cheerful tone that sounded fake to her. "Want something to eat?"

"I'd rather have it as a picnic."

"What?"

"Howard said I could go outside as long as someone went with me."

"True."

"Will you? I'd like to check the horses we delivered to make sure they're doing okay."

She was astonished at how his expression altered again, and candid entreaty appeared on his guarded face. She shouldn't have been surprised. A man who spent his whole day outdoors must be going stir-crazy stuck inside.

"I'll get the wheelchair." When he grimaced and started to protest he could manage on crutches, she said, "No chair, no going outside."

He scowled. "I'm not one of your kids."

"No, they would have figured out the only way to get what they want is to cooperate." She chuckled. "Or devised a way to distract me long enough for them to sneak outside."

"Is that what you think I should do? Distract you?"

She looked away. Didn't he know how much he beguiled her every time she was near him? The thought of putting her arm around his sturdy back again while she assisted him into the chair made her knees rubbery.

"Eat, and I'll get the chair." She'd use any excuse to get out of the room before she couldn't control her unsteady legs.

By the time Sarah returned with the wheelchair, Toby had eaten half of the roast-beef sandwich and finished the potato salad. She was relieved when he asked her to hold the chair steady; then, grasping its arms, he swung himself into it. Was he aware of the sensations that rushed between them, too?

The chair moved along the smooth floors as she wheeled him through the kitchen. Mrs. Beebe looked up from her work with a smile. On the other side of the vast room, two workmen were unpacking the new cabinets, which appeared to be a lot like the ones in place, only a few shades lighter.

"Are they replacing the cabinets?" asked Toby.

"Ja."

"They look pretty much the same."

"I know." She'd taken the job at the Summerhays house, in part, to help her learn more about *Englischers*, but she was more confused than the day she'd started.

A workman held the door open for them, and Sarah pushed the chair outdoors. Toby drew in a deep breath. She smiled, knowing he felt as if he'd escaped a closed box. Neither of her brothers liked being inside, either, preferring to work at their sawmill or in the fields or among the trees they planned to sell for Christmas.

If he was surprised the house had a ramp, Toby didn't say anything. Had he guessed the ramp had been built to allow renovation supplies to be moved more easily into the house? Or—and she suspected this was the truth—he was so eager to get out to where he could see the horses he didn't notice anything else.

The ground was rough, but Toby didn't complain each time the wheelchair pitched or halted. When Mick, a stableman, rushed to help, Sarah let him push the chair. Toby peppered the man with question after question until Mick glanced at Sarah and shrugged.

Knowing her patient wouldn't rest until he got the answers he needed, Sarah had Mick push the chair close to the paddock fence. She went around to the gate and inside. With Mick's help, she got a halter on the big horse and a lead rope hooked to him in less than ten minutes.

"Howdy, Bay Boy," called Toby.

The horse's ears pricked, and his head swung toward the fence. Sarah had to skip several times to keep up with him. Putting his head over the fence, he tried to reach Toby, a familiar voice and scent among the strange ones.

When Toby patted Bay Boy's nose, the horse nickered.

"He misses you, too," Sarah said.

At her voice, Bay Boy turned to her. She put out her hand for him to sniff, and she smiled when his chin whiskers tickled her skin.

"He seems to have taken a liking to you." Toby was smiling at her as if the horse's opinion mattered more to him than any human's. Most likely that was true.

She stroked the horse's face. "He's a *gut* boy. Mick says he's settling in well."

"I'm happy to hear that." His grin widened, amazing her. "Or are you telling me if a horse can settle in to new circumstances, I should be able to?"

"If the horseshoe fits—"

"Got it!" He stretched forward to touch the horse again.

Moving aside to give the two room, she listened as he spoke to Bay Boy as if the big stallion could comprehend every word. When Mick brought the other two horses, Toby greeted them, too. Her "patient" looked more relaxed than she'd ever seen him. Maybe now that he was reassured the horses were okay, he'd focus on his recovery.

Then he'd leave, and she wouldn't find herself paying too much attention to a plain man. That attraction could be another thing to come between her and her dreams of studying medicine. That must never happen.

Chapter Six

Sarah stood at the bottom of the porch steps. She made sure she could jump forward, but wouldn't step on the flowers blooming in front of the porch. Flowers that weren't poisonous to horses. Any bush or plant that might harm the valuable animals had been banished from the farm.

At the top of the steps, Toby was rising from the wheelchair he despised. Not that he'd complained, but his upper lip had a tendency to curl whenever the chair was mentioned.

She was surprised at his reaction. She'd thought, when she'd first brought him the wheelchair, he'd be pleased. It allowed him to get around the house and outdoors, though no farther than the porch or the ramp, because he couldn't maneuver alone across the uneven ground.

Without asking, she rushed up the steps and lifted the crutches lying by the wheelchair. She handed them to him, and he gave her a silent nod.

The door opened. Childish voices poured out onto the porch.

Sarah prepared to step between Toby and the youngsters. In their excitement, they might bowl him over or even knock him off the porch.

"Stay where you are," a stern voice ordered.

Beyond the screen door, Mrs. Hancock stood. As always, she wore a prim gray suit. The skirt's hem was as long as Sarah's dress. Her black hair was swept in a French twist, and she wore two pairs of glasses on glittering chains around her neck. An expensive watch peeked out from beneath her unadorned cuffs. It was a gift from Mrs. Summerhays after her previous trip to Europe.

Mrs. Hancock was not much taller than Sarah, but her aura of authority gave a first impression she had the stature of a giantess. Her family had lived in Salem since the village's founding in the late eighteenth century.

She frowned as she held back the two younger *kinder*, who were eager to come outside. Was she upset at the *kinder* or at Sarah, who was working with Toby? Either way, Sarah knew the housekeeper wasn't happy.

Toby looked over his shoulder and waved. The youngsters grinned as if they hadn't seen him in months instead of having breakfast with him that morning. When they called to him, he motioned for them to join them on the porch.

"Are you sure?" Sarah asked.

"I'd rather have them in my way than someone else's."

She smiled at how he'd phrased that so Mrs. Hancock's fragile feelings weren't hurt. Sarah called, "*Komm* out."

The *kinder* exploded from the house, swinging the screen door behind them.

"Whoa! No slamming the door." Sarah rushed to catch it in the *kinder's* wake.

Ethan and Mia glanced at each other as if finding it difficult to believe either of them could have been at fault.

When Sarah motioned for them to follow her down the steps, they complied.

She led them in the center of the walk. Putting a finger to her lips, she said, "We need to be quiet so Toby can concentrate on what he learned this morning."

The *kinder* had been busy with swimming lessons while Toby had his session with Howard. The physical therapist had to put a halt to the practice on the stairs because Toby wanted to keep going until he was proficient. Only the warning that every additional trip without a break to rest his ankle could do more damage to it had stopped Toby from trying "just one more time."

Making sure the youngsters wouldn't be in the way if Toby fell, Sarah signaled for Toby to start but halted him as he started to lower his left foot.

"That's wrong," she said.

"I made sure I've got my crutches under me before I moved." Impatience rippled through his protest.

"You can't lead with your foot. Remember? You put the crutches on each step before going down. Howard said that's important, so you keep your balance and don't tumble. He said you need to remember that until you can begin to put weight on your right foot." Sarah kept her tone light and wished Toby wouldn't act as if it were a life-and-death matter. "It shouldn't be hard to remember, ain't so?"

"Maybe not for you."

She refused to be drawn into an argument, so she said in her gentlest tone, "Lead with the *gut* foot going up, and then let the bad one swing through going down."

"Cuz good things go up and bad ones go down," said Mia and Ethan at the same time before Ethan added, "See? I remembered from when I broke my leg."

"So you did." She smiled at the *kinder*.

She had to keep her focus on Toby but knew how much mischief Ethan and Mia could get into as soon as her back was turned. Natalie and Alexander were having swimming lessons in the pool behind the house, and the teenager teaching them couldn't keep an eye on them as well as watch the younger *kinder*.

So she was grateful Toby was willing to have an audience while he did his afternoon exercises. After he worked on the steps, Sarah instructed Toby to write the alphabet with his right foot. Ethan and Mia copied him. They giggled when Mia made the letter *S* backward. The little girl started again and wore a proud grin when she did the letter correctly the second time.

Natalie stuck her head, which was wrapped in a colored beach towel, past the door. "Your turn now!"

"We want to help Toby," Mia argued. "I went swimming this morning."

"You know Mom wants us to be able to swim when we go to Aruba in January."

With a sigh that suggested she was sacrificing the most precious thing in the world, Mia shuffled after her brother.

The screen door slammed in their wake, and Toby glanced at Sarah.

She shrugged. "What's the point of reminding them not to slam the door *again* when they won't hear it?"

"It seems like they didn't hear it the first time."

"They did, but sometimes it takes a long time for an idea to go from the ears to the brain when those ears belong to someone six years old or younger." She smiled. "You've got to be patient."

"I'm not sure I could be."

"Why not? You're patient with your horses, aren't you?"

"That's different."

"How? You're teaching a horse to behave as you want. I'm doing the same with the *kinder*. In either case, we have to keep them safe as we teach them to behave without breaking their spirits."

He relaxed against his crutches and grinned. "I didn't realize our work had so much in common."

"It's strange, ain't so?" She moved to the walk and looked at him. "I'm ready when you are."

Sweat glistened on Toby's forehead by the time he went down the steps and then returned to his chair. She poured a glass of water from the pitcher she'd brought out with them.

Handing him the glass, she said, "You did it."

"*Ja*, but I should be doing better than this by now."

Sarah gave Toby the stern look that worked best with the Summerhays *kinder*. He ignored it and instead glowered at his right foot.

"It's only been two days," she said, hoping being reasonable would help.

It didn't.

"Two days of doing these exercises again and again. What have I gotten for it? I still can't put my weight on my right ankle."

"Two whole days?" She gave him an expression of feigned shock. He wanted a pity party. At least, that was the term Alexander had used when he complained about how Toby wouldn't do anything but grouse last night during supper.

She'd guessed that Toby would appreciate coming out to the small breakfast room where the *kinder* had their meals. Not only would he get practice with his crutches, but he'd have an excuse to leave his room.

She couldn't have been more mistaken. Toby hadn't

said more than a couple of words. Though she guessed his meds were making it difficult for him to think, he could have taken Mia's and Alexander's hands when they bowed their heads to say grace.

"I thought you'd have more sympathy for me," he grumbled.

"I've got plenty of sympathy for you, but not as much as you have for yourself. Maybe you'd rather be a race-horse," she fired back. "With an injury like this, the kind thing would be to put the horse down."

"I see what you're doing."

"Getting you to stop feeling sorry for yourself."

"With reverse psychology. It may work with the kids, but it won't work with me."

She gave a terse laugh. "I guess it won't, though I don't know what you're talking about. I guess you'd rather be a horse so you could be put out of your misery. And put the rest of us out of your misery, too."

"Okay, I'll put a positive spin on it, if that's what you want."

She sat on the other chair and faced him, wondering if all Amish men were *dikk-keppich*. As stubborn as a pair of mules. Her brothers were hardheaded when they wanted to get their way, as they had been that morning when they cut her off in the middle of her explanation of how she was helping with Toby's physical therapy so they could remind her they'd forbidden her to study medical matters.

Frustration threatened to overwhelm her. Why had Menno and Benjamin jumped to the conclusion her story was aimed at making them change their minds? It hadn't been her intention, and she was annoyed they thought she was trying to find a way around their edict. If they suspected she was considering leaving the community...

No, she didn't want to think about that. Better to focus on Toby and his sense of futility than her own.

"What positive spin could there be?" he asked, and she realized she'd been lost too long in thought.

"When you're training a horse, you don't expect it to be able to master everything you need it to learn in two days, ain't so?"

"I'm not a horse."

Irritated, she snapped, "No, you're acting more like a donkey!"

Toby watched Sarah's eyes widen as her face paled before turning as red as her hair. She hadn't meant to call him a donkey. Not that he could fault her. He knew he was being unreasonable, but he was tired of doing simple exercises that didn't bring perceivable improvement.

When she started to apologize, he waved her words away. "You don't need to ask forgiveness for the truth. I have been acting like a stubborn old donkey, braying and kicking." He gave her a wry grin. "Well, maybe not kicking. I'm not used to doing nothing and still being exhausted."

"Are you tired now?" she asked.

Ja, he wanted to shout. He was tired of being an invalid. He was tired of being dependent on others for things he'd done without thinking a week ago. Most of all, he was tired of being inside unless Sarah had the time to take him out to the porch.

He looked at the stairs to the yard. Three steps shouldn't be a barrier between him and the stables. But without someone to help him, the stables might as well be on the far side of the moon.

When Sarah put gentle fingers on his arm, he was shocked. He'd seen her offer a consoling hand to the *kinder*, but he hadn't expected her to treat him with the same familiarity. Or for his heartbeat to erupt into high gear at the light pressure of her warm skin against him.

"I'm sorry nothing is turning out as you'd hoped," she said. "I know how difficult that is."

Did she? Had she been thwarted in doing the simplest things as he was? Or, he wondered, was she referring to what made her eyes dim? He was curious what it was Sarah wanted to do when she seemed so content living in the new community with friends she would have for the rest of her life. The longing for roots among plain folk gripped him, but he pushed it aside with disgust. He had his home at J.J.'s ranch. Even the thought of moving somewhere could lead to the nomad life he'd had with his parents.

He aimed his glower at the wheelchair. "Do you know what I hate most? That chair, because if I want to go anywhere beyond the house, I need someone to push me."

"You don't like others pushing you around?"

He gave her a scowl in response to her smile, then felt horrible when her twinkling eyes grew dull. "I'm sorry, Sarah. You're trying to lift my spirits, and I'm acting as if I want you to be as miserable as I am."

"If that's not what you want, then what is?"

"I want to be able to work." He leaned toward her. "I suspect you'd be as impatient as I am if our situations were reversed."

"You're wrong."

"You rush about, chasing the *kinder* and taking care of them. If—"

"You didn't let me finish. If our situations were reversed, I'd be more impatient than you are."

A laugh bubbled inside him for the first time since... He couldn't remember the last time he'd laughed, and he wasn't going to today. Laughter was another invisible thread weaving people together, which was why he'd avoided it.

Pushing the laughter into the dark place deep in his heart where it'd been locked away, he saw she was waiting for his reaction. *Sever any chance of connection*, ordered the quiet, but annoying, voice that had first sounded in his mind after his *daed* had come home and insisted they prepare to move, right after twelve-year-old Toby had asked the cutest eleven-year-old girl in his school to sit with him during recess the next day. They never had that chance to sit together. In fact, he never saw her again.

That leave-taking had been the one to persuade him—at last—that he'd be a fool to make friends again. He counted the men who worked for J.J. as acquaintances. Most didn't stay long but went looking for other work, or whatever they wanted for their lives.

Sarah sat straighter, drawing his eyes to her. "You're like the Summerhays kids. If there's something you don't want to do, you need a goal to convince yourself to do it."

"What I need to do is be able to walk."

She laughed, shocking him. He hadn't guessed she'd be the type to find humor in someone else's pain.

Stop it! She wasn't laughing at him. Because he didn't want to be beholden to her wasn't her fault.

Making sure his voice didn't reveal the tumult inside him, he asked, "Okay, what is this goal you've got in mind?"

"Something you'd enjoy and what might make your stay here feel as if it's been worthwhile."

A kiss? He tried to smother that thought, but it popped into his head as he admired how her brown eyes glowed behind her gold-rimmed glasses.

"Aren't you curious what I've got in mind?" she asked.

"What?"

"If before the racing season ends at Saratoga next month, in the *doktor's* opinion—not yours—your ankle can handle the exertion, I'll ask Mr. Summerhays to arrange for you to spend a day at his stables there." She grinned as she asked, "How's that for a goal? Enough of a challenge for you, cowboy?"

He was astonished how she'd discovered the exact carrot to hold out as incentive for him to work even harder. His efforts to keep a wall between them had been futile. She was able to see within him to know what he'd prize.

Happiness flowed through him, as gentle and inviting as her smile when he replied, "I'm not a cowboy. I'm a groom. A horse trainer."

"So?"

"So this horse trainer is going to accept your goal. You'll see. I'll make it happen."

"I hope you do."

As she put her fingers on his forearm again and gave it a kind squeeze, he realized she meant what she'd said.

He was getting in too deep with her and the Summerhays family, but, for once, he didn't retreat. He was leaving as soon as he healed. They knew that, so why not enjoy a challenge—and her sweet smile and enticing touch—until then?

Chapter Seven

It wasn't right to be proud of being able to lean at the same time on his crutches and on the top rail of the fence around the pasture where Bay Boy had been turned out while his stall was being cleaned. But Toby was. With the crutches holding him, he folded his arms on the fence and stood as if his ankle had never been hurt.

At last, he was where he belonged. No longer a complete invalid.

He watched the big horse's gait with a practiced eye. Bay Boy showed no sign of favoring one leg as he'd seemed to on the trailer during the ride from Texas. Had the horse been faking an injury, or had it been so minor it had healed?

Without getting closer to the horse, he wouldn't be able to tell. The *doktor* and Howard had instructed him—and Sarah—that Toby must stay away from horses and view them from the far side of the fence until he could walk without crutches. The sight of the metal crutches might spook Bay Boy again.

Toby had to admit the precaution made sense, but he didn't have to like it. After more than a week and a half of doing exercises and spending too much of his time doing little more than sitting, he was itching to work with Bay Boy.

"Whatcha doing?" asked Natalie as she trotted to where he stood.

She wore bright pink shorts with polka dots and a garish orange shirt with a stylized cat on it. Her hair looked as if it hadn't been brushed, and neither her sneakers nor her socks matched.

"Watching Bay Boy. Does Sarah know you're out here?" He'd seen the girl wandering into the stables earlier but had figured she'd found something else to do by now. The grooms had mentioned there were two litters of kittens hiding in the hay stored behind the main building. If Natalie had been looking for them, she must have given up.

Natalie shrugged. "Sarah didn't get here early enough. If she wants me, she knows where to find me. She knows I love horses."

He translated that to mean Natalie had slipped out of the house before Sarah had arrived for the day. He waited for the irritation he expected to feel when realizing that he should keep an eye on the girl until Sarah came looking for her. It didn't buzz through him, and he was surprised to discover he was curious why the girl had sought him out.

Natalie scrambled to the top of the rail fence with an ease he had to envy. At times, it seemed as if it'd been someone else, instead of him, who used to be able to scale fences with ease. His hands could recall the firm, rough strength of a wooden rail beneath them as he vaulted over.

He grinned. Maybe Sarah was right. In some ways, he didn't act older than the kids who needed a goal to work hard. He should have laughed along with her when she'd said that. As he imagined laughing with her, seeing her eyes crinkle, he knew he'd been a fool to resist the impulse when they'd been sitting together on the porch last week. It was better in the long run that he hadn't, but letting the moment go past felt like a loss.

"He's special, ain't so?" Natalie asked.

He smiled at the phrase she'd learned from Sarah. "I think he could be."

"Bay Boy is strong." Her gaze followed the powerful horse galloping around the pasture. "Have you been working with him long?"

"About a year and a half, though I started training him when he wasn't much more than a foal."

"Did you start him off with a halter or a lead?"

He looked at the young girl beside him. She spoke with the authority and knowledge of a seasoned groom. "A lead."

"That's good."

"*Ja*, I agree. But why do you think so?"

Not taking her gaze from the horse, she said, "A lead lets the horse see you at the same time you're teaching it to listen to your commands." She leaned forward to rest her elbows on her knees, shifting to keep her balance on the top rail. "Horses don't like surprises. If you want them to trust you, you can't surprise them."

"That's true." He waited, wanting to gauge if she knew what she was talking about or just repeating what she'd heard in the barn.

"Bay Boy is special," she said again.

"Why do you think that?"

"He's well built, and he eats like a teenager." She grinned. "Daddy said so on the phone." Her smile vanished as she looked at the horse.

Guessing she wasn't supposed to be eavesdropping

on her *daed's* calls, Toby replied, "Eating well is important, ain't so?"

She smiled again. "Running is hard, and if he doesn't eat a lot, he can't run fast. He's calm." She glanced toward his bandaged ankle. "Getting scared by a cat doesn't count."

"No, it doesn't."

"He's going to be the best." The girl continued to list the reasons Bay Boy would make a great racer.

He listened, impressed with her insight, though he shouldn't have been surprised. The few times he'd seen Summerhays since his arrival, Natalie's *daed* seldom spoke of anything other than the horses in his stables and his hopes for them. *Kinder* soaked up everything they heard…even things adults didn't realize they'd overheard.

"*Ach*, here you are!" came Sarah's voice from behind them.

Natalie jumped from the fence, her smile vanishing. The girl nodded but didn't hide a rebellious expression when Sarah reminded her she should have let someone in the house know where she was going.

"I know," Natalie said.

"*Gut*. Now hurry inside. Your French tutor is waiting for you."

The girl muttered, *"Je déteste parler français!"* Her words were understandable to Toby, who knew no French but could read her body language. Her distaste for her lessons was as clear as if she'd shouted it. She stamped toward the house.

He turned to Sarah and couldn't help smiling when he saw how the morning sunshine glowed off her downy cheeks. As always, that single strand of bright red hair refused to stay pinned beneath her *kapp*, and it edged her cheek to accent its gentle curve.

"How many times do you have to repeat the same thing before they listen?" asked Toby as Sarah pushed the vagrant hair into place.

"I'll let you know when I find out." She sighed. "It's not easy to scold them when they're doing what kids do."

"Did you say she's learning French? During the summer? Did she fall behind in her work during school?"

"No, Natalie is very smart. All four *kinder* have regular lessons. Language, swimming, dance, gymnastics, art classes."

"When do they have time to play?"

She grimaced. "On rare occasions, and when they do, they don't seem to know how to play the games our *kinder* do. They tend to go looking for trouble inside instead of finding a game to enjoy outside. They're learning foreign languages and how to swim, but not how to play."

"That's sad."

"I've been teaching them tag and a few other outdoors games." She walked to the fence and looked at Bay Boy and the other horses that had been let out with him. "Ah, now I see what lured Natalie out here. She loves everything about horses."

"Does Summerhays realize how much she knows?"

"I don't think anyone can be unaware of it. Natalie breathes and sleeps and dreams and talks endlessly about horses." Her smile faded as the girl's had, and for a moment, Sarah seemed as wistful as Natalie had while talking about Bay Boy. "I wish…"

"You wish what?"

Her battle with herself was visible on her face. She wanted to say something but was unsure if she should.

He halted himself from telling her she could trust him, that he wouldn't repeat what she said. Doing so would create another strand connecting them together. He had to figure out a way to pull apart the ones in place, not make more.

If she was aware of his struggle, there was no sign of it in her voice as she replied, "The *kinder* are eager to spend more time with their parents, but Mr. and Mrs. Summerhays are busy with other aspects of their lives. They don't offer their *kinder* much other than a nice home and plenty to eat, nice clothes to wear and educational experiences. You haven't been upstairs, but Natalie must have close to a hundred plastic and porcelain horses on shelves in her room. The other kids have as many toys, and there are enough books for a public library. They've got everything they need, just not what they want."

"So what are you going to do about it?"

Sarah closed her mouth that had gaped at Toby's forthright question. What was *she* going to do about the youngsters' longing to spend more time with their parents? From what she'd learned from Natalie, Ian and Jessica Summerhays had concentrated on their own lives for as long as the *kind* could remember. At first, Natalie as Jessica's daughter and Alexander as Ian's son had believed their parents would pay more attention to them after they were married. Nothing changed, though, even when Ethan and Mia were born. The girl said she and her siblings had hoped a move from New York City to Washington County two years ago would mean their *daed* wouldn't have to work endless hours and their *mamm* would spend more time with them.

Again, nothing changed. In fact, their *daed* was frequently gone overnight to New York City for business meetings, and their *mamm* seemed to come home only long enough to unpack and repack for her next trip.

Sarah had no doubts the parents loved their *kinder*,

because they'd asked many questions during her job interview, and Mr. Summerhays had insisted on a background check. Each time either parent traveled, they brought home *wunderbaar* gifts for the *kinder*. They never seemed to comprehend that what their kids wanted most was time with them.

"Well?" he prompted when she didn't answer. "You're here for a reason, aren't you?"

"Ja." She'd applied for the job to help her brothers pay the bills while they made their sawmill, Christmas tree business and their few fertile fields profitable.

That wasn't what Toby meant. God must have brought her to this family for a reason. Could it have been to help the *kinder* by assisting their parents to see how much they were missing in not spending time with the mischievous quartet? The kids had done everything they could, being so outrageous she couldn't imagine what they'd do next, in an effort to get their parents to notice them.

Leaning her elbows on the fence, she said, "I've got to think about how to approach Mr. and Mrs. Summerhays."

"With the truth is the best way. They've pretty much handed their responsibility for their *kinder* to you and the others working in the house."

"I realize that." She wished her brothers would be a bit more like Ian and Jessica Summerhays, instead of judging everything she said and did as if she were as untrustworthy as a toddler. "However, I don't want to upset them so much they'll get angry. If I get fired, I won't be able to help further."

He gave her a wry grin. "You won't get fired. From what I've heard, the *kinder* have chased away every other nanny before you. One didn't stay a full day. Until you came along, the longest stint of any nanny was less than a month. Short of rustling Mr. Summerhays's favorite horses, I can't imagine anything you could do that would get you fired."

Sarah had to admit he was right. Within hours of her first day at the house, she'd realized her main job was to keep the *kinder's* parents from worrying about their offspring. But it still didn't feel right to speak about Mr. and Mrs. Summerhays when they weren't there to defend themselves.

When she told him that, his shoulders relaxed from their taut lines. "To be honest, I wasn't sure how you'd take my advice."

"I want to help this family."

"I know. They are like your family at this point."

"They are." She turned to head into the house, then paused. "We're having church this Sunday. Would you like to *komm*?"

"I don't have a way to get there."

"Of course you do. I'll come by. It's not more than about a ten-minute drive from my house." She chuckled. "Not that I drive often, because it's quicker if I cut through the woods and the fields between our farm and the stables."

She was sure he was going to say no, so she was amazed when he replied, "I'll go with you."

"*Gut.* Our services start at eight, so I'll be here about a half hour before." She faced him. "I'm glad you'll be joining us."

"As I'm going to be here another month, it'll be nice to meet your neighbors."

"Our *Leit* is welcoming."

"As you've been with an injured man who's added to your responsibilities."

"I haven't minded." She looked forward to talking with him.

"I see how much you love taking care of these *kinder*. Anyone who spends more than a few seconds in this house can see how important this job is to you. That's why I half expected you to tell me to mind my business."

"I wouldn't do that."

"No, I suppose you wouldn't, but, Sarah, I want *you* to know I wouldn't suggest anything to endanger your job. I know how important it is to you."

She stiffened, biting her tongue. Toby couldn't mean his words the way she was hearing them. She didn't want to believe he was being overprotective like her brothers and as Wilbur had. Toby wasn't telling her what to do. He was being honest as he tried to help her make the best decision.

Right?

She wished she could be sure about that, but she wasn't going to make the same mistake again and let another man think she needed his help to keep her from making mistakes.

Chapter Eight

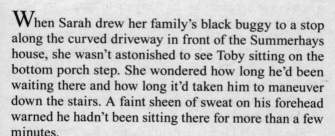

When Sarah drew her family's black buggy to a stop along the curved driveway in front of the Summerhays house, she wasn't astonished to see Toby sitting on the bottom porch step. She wondered how long he'd been waiting there and how long it'd taken him to maneuver down the stairs. A faint sheen of sweat on his forehead warned he hadn't been sitting there for more than a few minutes.

Nobody would be awake in the house before eight on a Sunday morning. It was the one day Mr. Summerhays slept late, and the *kinder* knew to be quiet until he woke. She'd seen motions in the stables, but those had been slow and she guessed whoever was tending to the horses wished he was still in bed.

Climbing out of the buggy, she watched Toby push himself up and rest his weight on the crutches. His dark coat had buttons. It must have belonged to Mr. Summerhays. With it, he wore a simple white shirt and his jeans and boots.

Lifting a folded *mutze* coat and vest out of the buggy, she handed them to Toby. "These should fit."

"*Danki.*" He shed his coat. The vest and the coat were

a bit taut across the chest, but he was able to close them with the hooks and eyes. When she held out a black felt hat, he asked, "Where did you get these?"

"They belong to my brother Benjamin. He's the taller of my brothers, so I figured there was a chance the clothes might fit you. Neither of them will be attending church this morning. They've got two cows in labor, and one had a tough time with her last calf. Or so they were told when they bought her."

Taking his other borrowed coat, she draped it over a chair on the porch. She turned toward him and pressed a hand over her heart as she tried not to gasp.

Toby was settling the hat, which was a bit small, on his head. It completed his transformation. Gone was the *Englisch*-looking horse trainer, and in his place was an Amish man. The black clothing contrasted with the streaks of gold in his hair falling along the standing collar of the coat, emphasizing the paler color as well as the shadowed crags of his face.

She was glad her face didn't display her shock. Or at least he didn't seem to notice as he made his way on his crutches toward the buggy.

"Nice horse," he said as he paused by the horse that was the same black as the buggy. "Slim, but with strong legs."

"Charmer came with us from Indiana."

"Charmer?"

"It was part of the much longer name Charmer had before he was retired from training to become a racehorse." She stroked the horse's nose. "That way, we didn't have to teach him another name." She smiled at the big horse. "Charmer is a charming guy. Somehow, he can smell an apple a mile away and, as soon as he knows it's nearby, he always manages to get his teeth on it. Not by stealing it or begging. Just by looking adoring and pitiful at the same time so you can't help but give him the apple."

"Sort of like Mia, who finds a way to get her hands on the last cookie."

She shook her head. "No, more like Alexander. Mia is young, so she's not as aware of what she's doing as her big brother is. Be careful if either he or Natalie start complimenting you. They're sure to ask for a favor afterward."

"So it's not just me they see as an easy mark?"

"*Ach!* I didn't realize they'd tried something with you."

"Last night they began to talk about how *gut* the ice cream is at the shop in the village. Wouldn't it be a shame, they pondered at length, if someone as kind and generous as I am didn't have the opportunity to try it before I left Salem?"

"That sounds like their usual style. Did you give in?"

"No, though I helped them raid the refrigerator to find pie from supper."

When she laughed, she listened for him to join in. He didn't. She'd never heard him laugh, though he smiled more each passing day.

Instead, he reached to climb into the passenger side of the buggy. "*Gut* foot first." He smiled.

When his eyes sparkled like stars admiring themselves in a deep pond, every bit of oxygen seemed to vanish from her lungs. She was aware of his strong arm draped across her shoulders and his lean leg pressed against her skirt. They'd been close many times during his physical therapy sessions, but standing within the arc of his arm now seemed so intimate.

He lifted himself into the buggy, and she handed him his crutches without looking at him. Hurrying around the buggy to get in herself, she took the reins.

The clatter of driveway gravel against the metal wheels

was loud. Once they reached the paved road, the horse-shoes and the wheels combined to make a resonant sound that followed them toward the road leading into the hollow. She steered the buggy around a large pothole. Though Charmer would have skirted it, he didn't always keep the buggy behind him in mind.

Beside her, Toby was silent as he scanned the fields and the foothills rising to the Green Mountains to the east. The lush foliage layered the hillsides in every possible shade of green. She wondered how the view compared with Texas's hill country, but she didn't want to intrude into his thoughts.

Each time new questions filled her head, she realized how little she knew about Toby Christner. Somehow, he straddled the two worlds, Amish and *Englisch*, in a way she hadn't managed. She wanted to ask him how he did it, but to voice her curiosity might disclose her uncertainty about remaining Amish. She couldn't speak of that to anyone, because she didn't want her brothers discovering she was thinking of becoming *Englisch*.

He brushed sweat away from his temple. "If it's hot this early in the day..."

"It's going to be another scorcher." She smiled in his direction. "Of course, you must have a lot of days like this in southern Texas."

"That doesn't mean I like them." He lifted off the black hat and ran his fingers along the inner band. "Today isn't the day for a wool hat."

"Do you wear straw ones to services in Texas?"

He shook his head. "No, but it would be a *gut* idea."

"Maybe you should mention it to your bishop."

"He dragged his feet for a long time when the *Leit* voted to use solar panels for their local businesses. He's a fine man but doesn't like change." He looked away.

"Not that I've gone to services much. Whose house are we going to?"

His question warned her he didn't want to talk about why he hadn't joined others on a church Sunday.

"The Bowmans," she replied. "David is a widower with two school-age boys. Their *grossmammi* takes care of the boys and the house. Here we are."

She pulled into the driveway leading to a well-cared-for white farmhouse. The barn behind it was smaller than on the other farms they'd passed, but it was sufficient for the ever-increasing flock of sheep David was raising. Wide grassy pastures led to foothills behind the house. Though the farm had the same number of acres as her family's farm, it appeared much larger because the hills around her home were covered with trees.

"There are a bunch of different buggies here." He pointed to where a half-dozen buggies were parked beneath a large maple.

"We've come to this new settlement from various districts and states. It was voted during the discussions on our new *Ordnung* that we'll use gray buggies like the ones from Lancaster County in Pennsylvania."

"But yours is black."

"We're from Indiana. The changeover won't start until after the harvest is finished."

"So every family can contribute something to pay for new buggies?"

She wasn't surprised he understood. Helping one another in a community was common among the plain people. "*Ja.* These other buggies will be sold or remade into vehicles we can use. Some may become open buggies. The Troyers' Delaware buggy will become our bench wagon to take supplies from house to house for church Sundays."

"How far along are you on your *Ordnung*?"

"We've discussed most issues. Buggies and clothing were first and the simplest. Last week, when we met, the focus was on what equipment can be used on the farms. Having diesel engines to power milk tanks was approved at that meeting, but we need to have more discussion about skid steers to move bales of hay or other heavy items."

He shifted his right leg with care. "I never thought about how many details there can be in an *Ordnung*."

"I don't think we realized how long it would take, but we're making progress. We hope to have it in place before communion Sunday in October so we can ordain our first leaders."

She didn't add more because her neighbors waved and called greetings. She saw the interest in everyone's eyes and knew they were eager to meet Toby. The Wagler twins stood to one side. Sarah realized Toby wouldn't be the only one fielding plenty of questions.

Toby was welcomed by the district's men as if he were a longtime member of the community. Nobody asked questions about where he lived or what he was doing in Harmony Creek Hollow. Instead, they were curious to learn how his ankle was healing and how the horses he'd brought with him were faring.

For a moment, he was leery. What had the Amish grapevine along Harmony Creek shared about him? That he was stubborn? That he was from Texas? That his *daed's* assumption he knew more than anyone else had disrupted every district they'd lived in? Recalling how Sarah had said the people in the Harmony Creek settlement came from many districts, was it possible someone living here had once been in a community he and his family had joined temporarily?

He calmed himself. Nobody spoke of the past. The men were talking about the harvest. One mentioned the dearth of canning jars and how his wife had sent him to the next town to purchase some, which brought questions about where the jars had been found. Everyone who had a garden was now reaping the results of a summer taking care of the plants.

As the men gathered to go into the barn for the service to begin, Toby found himself in the middle. He worried about slowing others but managed to keep up with the elderly man in front of him.

The benches, set so the men would face the women during the service, were familiar and welcoming. He'd gotten out of the habit of attending services in Texas, and he'd forgotten the warmth of worshipping with others. In astonishment, he realized everyone in the barn, the men sitting on the backless benches and the women and *kinder* coming in to take their seats, were newcomers. Every other service he'd ever attended had been filled with people who'd been born, raised, and would die in that district.

No wonder nobody asked about his past. Everyone along Harmony Creek was interested in the present and the future they planned to build together.

Through the service, led by the bishop from a more established settlement thirty miles to the north, Toby had to struggle to keep his gaze from Sarah, who sat across from him. She was keeping a toddler entertained with a handkerchief that she'd tied to look like a bunny or a cat. The *kind's mamm* sat beside her, holding what looked to be a new *boppli*.

Sarah drew his eyes again and again. She looked somber as she listened to the sermons, but an aura of joy surrounded her as she cradled the toddler, who'd fallen asleep, in her arms. Being with *kinder* made her as happy as he was when he spent time with horses. They were blessed to have found jobs that gave them satisfaction.

He couldn't help noticing, though, how several other men glanced in her direction. He guessed, when she was ready to marry, she'd have her choice among her bachelor neighbors. Instead of a *gut* feeling of knowing someone who'd done so much for him would have a great future, his stomach knotted at the thought.

Had he lost his mind? *He* wasn't going to bind his life to someone who could tear him away from what he wanted to do and where he wanted to be. Maybe Sarah would settle in Harmony Creek Hollow for the rest of her life, but maybe not. She and her brothers had moved from Indiana. That was the way it had started with his parents. They'd lived their whole youths in one district, but then once they'd moved a single time, it seemed they had never hesitated to do so again. Would Sarah be the same?

He tried to focus on the sermon, because the bishop was an inspired speaker, but his thoughts kept creeping toward Sarah. When the service was finished, he watched when she went to speak with three other young women on their way to the house to bring food for the shared meal.

Again, Toby was made to feel welcome by the men, who were interested in the techniques he used to train horses. Nobody pressured him about his past or his future, and the subject again turned to the harvest and the volunteer work many of the younger men did with the local first responders. He found it fascinating, but his eyes cut too often to Sarah. If the others took note, they said nothing.

As soon as the women and *kinder* had eaten and the

dishes were cleared away, she walked toward him. He thought she was ready to leave, until he realized she wasn't alone. The woman walking beside Sarah had midnight-black hair and dark brown eyes.

Sarah introduced him to Mercy Bamberger, who wore an identical *kapp* to hers, before adding, "Mercy is attending the class for this fall's baptism."

"Ja." She spoke as if trying out each word. "I grew up a Mennonite, and I'm learning what I need to in order to join this community."

"We can speak in *Englisch*," he said.

"No, no," she urged, continuing haltingly in *Deitsch*. "I need practice. My kids speak it better than I do, and they laugh at my mistakes. Nothing like *kinder* to keep you from suffering from *hochmut*."

Sarah laughed. "That's a lesson I learn anew every day when I'm with the Summerhays *kinder*. Just when I think I've convinced them to do something the right way, they show me that they can figure out more ways to *not* do it."

"I'd like to pick your brain, Sarah, for ideas to keep *kinder* entertained," Mercy replied, "once my summer camp is running."

"A summer camp?" he asked.

"We plan to open next summer. It's for city kids to have a week or two in the country."

"I've heard of such programs, but I didn't think the Amish would run one."

"With the bishop's permission, we're opening it on a trial basis next summer." She glanced at Sarah before adding, "That's why I wanted to talk to you, Toby. We're going to need gentle horses willing to be ridden by inexperienced riders."

He nodded. "Your riders will be nervous, so your horses must remain calm."

"Would you be willing to look at a few horses I may buy for the camp?" She glanced at his crutches. "If it's too much, feel free to say so. Jeremiah is so busy with getting in the harvest I hesitate to ask him. However, I want to get the horses moved soon so they're accustomed to us before the first *kind* arrives."

"Where are the horses?"

"At a farm in West Hebron. It's on the other side of Salem. About ten miles from here." She turned to Sarah. "What is the name of the van driver you use?"

"Did you sell your car?" she asked.

Mercy nodded. "A couple of days ago." She smiled in Toby's direction. "I don't miss not having electricity, but I miss having a car and jumping into it whenever I need to go somewhere."

"Jeremiah says you're getting much better driving a horse." Sarah gave her a warm smile.

"At least I'm driving the horse instead of the other way around."

"There's a phone in the barn. I can call Hank and see if he's available to drive us to West Hebron tomorrow."

When Sarah excused herself, Toby continued talking with Mercy about the camp. Each word she spoke amazed him more, because he couldn't imagine his bishop in Texas allowing anyone in his districts to open a camp for *Englisch kinder* who lived in big cities.

Sarah returned before he could ask more. "Tomorrow won't work. Hank has appointments all day."

Mercy's smile wobbled. "I'll just wait until after school starts. *Danki*, Toby, for being willing to join us."

"Let me ask Mr. Summerhays if we can use his truck," Sarah said. "It's got plenty of room." She faltered. "It'll depend on having someone able to drive us."

"I can drive," he said.

Sarah frowned. "You sprained your right ankle. Don't you need your right foot to drive?"

"If it's an automatic—"

"It is."

"Then I can use my left foot." He grinned. "I've had to do that sometimes when working in the fields."

Mercy looked from Sarah to him. "Aren't you Amish, Toby?"

"I was raised that way, but I haven't made decisions about the future yet." He clamped his lips closed. He'd said too much.

Far too much, he realized, when he watched Sarah's eyes widen.

Sarah silenced the questions she wanted to ask. Why was Toby sitting on the fence as she was, trying to decide which side to jump to? He could continue to do the work he loved with training horses if he was baptized, though he'd be proscribed from driving. That alone wouldn't cause him to hesitate, would it? There must be another reason.

Toby kept so much to himself. He talked about horses, but his past was lost in a haze that was impossible to penetrate. Several times, she'd noticed him halt himself from speaking. He was a private man, and she respected that.

Somehow, she kept her curiosity to herself while they made arrangements to go to West Hebron the next day. When she got in the big red truck with Mercy and Toby the next day, she let the other two talk about the horses Mercy was interested in buying. If she opened her mouth, her questions might tumble out.

Sarah was grateful when they reached the farm nestled between two hills covered with pine trees. Unlike the ones

Benjamin had begun trimming in preparation for customers in a few months, these trees were tall and unsuitable for what *Englischers* sought for holiday decorating. The red outbuildings and the bright blue house were as tidy as an Amish farm. Clothing hung from the line, dancing in the light breeze, but unlike plain laundry, the clothes were decorated with a variety of patterns, buttons and zippers.

Toby stopped the truck and released the breath he'd been holding for the past five minutes while he'd driven the big truck along a twisting dirt road that seemed to be built of rocks and potholes. She didn't blame him. They'd been bounced about, and she guessed he hadn't been sure if, sitting at an odd angle to let himself drive with his left foot, he'd be able to control the big vehicle if it were tossed too far to one side or the other.

"Now I know what cream feels like in an ice-cream maker." Sarah settled her *kapp* in place as they got out of the truck.

"Spun about." Mercy smiled. "I'm glad you were driving, Toby, and not me. Thank the *gut* Lord, Mr. Fleetwood has offered to deliver the horses if I decide to buy."

A trio of small white dogs rushed toward them, barking an enthusiastic welcome. They halted and regarded Toby. A low growl came from one.

"They're leery of your crutches," said a man stepping out into the sunlight. He slapped a dark blue baseball cap on his bald head. "Frank Fleetwood. You are?" He offered his hand, his white mustache tilting with his smile.

Toby shook it as Mercy introduced him and Sarah to Mr. Fleetwood. The man's hands were ingrained with black.

As if they'd asked, the old man said, "I had a blacksmith shop for forty years, but I retired earlier this year.

Still getting the last of the soot out of my skin. I heard you Amish folks have a new smith coming to join you."

Sarah exchanged a glance with Mercy before saying, "I hadn't heard that, but I hope you're right. It can take several days for us to track down a farrier and get him out to replace a shoe."

"Hearing you say that makes me want to heat my old forge again, but the wife wouldn't appreciate that. She wants to travel more to see the grandkids in Georgia and Missouri, so I've hung up my tools." He shot Toby a wink. "If the rumors are true, let your new smith know I'm looking to sell my tools, so he's welcome to come and check them out."

"You should mention that to Jeremiah, Mercy," Toby said as they walked toward the pasture where a half-dozen horses grazed.

Sarah understood what he wasn't saying. He didn't want to be obliged to pass along the information…in case J.J. arrived sooner than planned.

When they reached the gate, Toby motioned for Sarah to come inside with him. "Help me here?"

"How?" she asked while Mr. Fleetwood went to lead the first horse, a dark brown gelding, toward them.

"Let me use you as a crutch for a moment."

She looked puzzled but nodded.

Leaving his crutches to lean against the rail, he put his hand on her shoulder. He hopped on his left foot and, with her to steady him, maneuvered himself so he was facing the horse, which the older man brought to stand near them.

She nodded again when Toby told her to copy his motions. She squatted when he did, each breath she took flavored with the mixed scents of horse and man, an aroma that would always remind her of this handsome man.

He slanted toward the horse, talking to it, and each motion brushed his muscular arm or leg against her. Focusing on what he was doing would have helped, but she couldn't stop from thinking about his inadvertent touch. He seemed oblivious, concentrating on his task. Why couldn't she be more like that?

Toby ran his hands along the horse's leg and frowned. "You need to have a vet look at this leg. It's swollen."

"Is that a problem?" asked Mercy.

He glanced at her. "It can be, or it can be something minor. It's important to make sure. I don't want you to get a horse you can't depend on." He patted the gelding and stood with Sarah's help. "I don't know, though, the last time I've seen a calmer horse. He should be *gut* with your city kids who aren't used to being around live animals. If he let me check his tender leg when he doesn't know me, he's not going to be bothered by someone who doesn't know how to sit in a saddle."

"He'll be good," Frank added, "if you want to do trail rides. He doesn't mind work, but he doesn't have much initiative. So don't make him the lead horse, and he'll do great." He grinned as he scratched the horse's nose. "Isn't that so, Cocoa?"

The horse bobbed its head as if it understood what the old man was saying.

Toby examined three more horses. One, though not young, shied away from his touch. That wouldn't do for a horse ridden by different *kinder* each week.

Mercy and Mr. Fleetwood agreed she'd buy Cocoa, after the vet checked him, and two other horses. While they discussed when the horses would be delivered to Mercy's farm, Sarah handed Toby his other crutch.

"*Danki* for helping Mercy get the best possible horses

for her camp," she said when they went to the truck to wait for Mercy.

"I like to help." He smiled at her, sending a trill of joyful music through her. "As you do."

Mercy interjected as she joined them, "You're two of a kind. I'm glad you were willing to give me your opinion today."

Toby smiled, but it wasn't a steady smile. Sarah understood, because Mercy's words pleased and disconcerted her. How alike were she and Toby? Really?

He made no secret of how eager he was to be gone from Harmony Creek Hollow and how he was straddling the fence between a plain life and an *Englisch* one; yet he hadn't made a decision where his future was. She was the same, though she'd miss her family and friends in the new settlement if she jumped the fence.

She guessed there was one major difference. More and more, she envisioned her future with Toby in it. Did he see her in his?

Chapter Nine

"Ready to go?" called Natalie as she bustled across the yard the next morning, herding her younger siblings toward the red truck.

Sarah stood by the passenger door while Cecil, a groom, sat behind the wheel.

"Can we stop for ice cream at the soda shop?" asked Alexander.

"Ice cream! Ice cream! Ice cream!" The youngest two grabbed each other's hands and began to dance about in a circle.

"Whoa!" At Toby's shout, the *kinder* froze and stared in astonishment. "Why do you expect Sarah to answer you when you aren't listening?"

His question startled the foursome into silence. Turning so the *kinder* couldn't see his playful wink, he walked to where she stood.

"Welcome to the chaos," she said with a chuckle.

"Looks as if you're going somewhere."

"To get haircuts for the *kinder*." She arched a brow. "I'm sure they can fit you in, if you'd like."

He touched his hair that now reached the bottom of his collar. "It looks bad?"

She was glad Ethan let out a shout at that moment. It kept her from having to devise a way to avoid answering Toby's question. The truth was he looked handsome with his hair curling along his nape. Going to separate the boys who were arguing whether chocolate or chocolate-chip ice cream was better gave her time to compose herself.

"*Komm* with us," she said as she motioned for the kids to climb into the back seat of the large pickup. "It'll give you a chance to see something other than this farm."

When he nodded, her heart did jumping jacks. She shouldn't be reacting so to a man who would be leaving soon, but today she wasn't going to worry. She was going to be grateful to have another adult along with her to deal with the *kinder*. She tried to convince herself that was the only reason she was happy he was joining them.

But she—and her eager heart—knew it wasn't the truth.

Veronica's Shearly Beloved Salon was one of two beauty shops along Main Street in Salem. The name came, Sarah informed Toby as they got out of the truck, from the fact that Veronica's husband was the pastor at the community church around the corner on West Broadway, and Veronica did the hair of many brides he married. The beauty salon was located in half of what had once been a grocery store, so it had high metal ceilings and, along one wall, the original shelves now held beauty products instead of canned vegetables and mayonnaise. Four chairs were set in front of a long mirror on the opposite wall, and sinks and dryers were arranged farther back.

Toby followed the Summerhays kids into the shop. It was, he was relieved to discover, only a pair of steps up from the sidewalk. His nose wrinkled. The odors of hair spray and permanent-wave solution filled each breath.

Every head turned as they entered. Two beauticians were talking by the front desk, three more were cleaning and a manicurist sat with an elderly female client at a small table half hidden by an artificial palm. At first, he thought the women were focused on the *kinder*; then he realized they were staring at him. Maybe, despite Sarah's offer, they didn't usually cut men's hair in the shop.

One beautician by the desk came to greet them. It was Veronica, and she wore her pure white hair in a bun resembling the one visible through Sarah's *kapp*. She bade the other women to come and collect the *kinder*. As they went to have their hair washed and Sarah followed, Veronica smiled at him.

"Are you here for a haircut, too?" she asked.

He nodded.

"Don't worry…"

"Toby," he supplied.

"Don't worry, Toby. You aren't a stranger in a strange land here. We do everyone's hair." She walked to the nearest chair. "Sit here. Do you need help getting into the chair?"

Shaking his head, he sat. He handed Veronica his crutches and leaned forward while she hooked a cape around his neck. When she asked where he was from, he told her.

"Texas?" she asked with a smile he saw reflected in the mirror. "You go for big hair down there."

He smiled, appreciating how she hadn't mentioned how he'd hobbled across the salon like a bird with a broken wing. "They say everything is bigger in Texas."

"Do you want something new or a trim?"

"A trim."

Sarah, who had come to stand between his chair and the one next to it where Mia now perched on a booster seat, bit her lower lip. Was she trying to keep from asking why he no longer wore the bowl cut he must have had as a *kind*? He didn't mind telling her he'd started having his hair cut in the *Englisch* style once he began working on J.J.'s ranch. It had helped make the other ranch hands forget he'd been raised Amish. He wasn't ashamed of his background. He just didn't want to have to answer the same awkward questions each time someone new was hired.

That was why he'd changed his look, ain't so?

He was shocked by an uncertainty he hadn't expected. *Was* he embarrassed that his past was different from the other ranch hands? No, he was grateful to have been raised plain. So why did he work hard to be like the rest of the world instead of separate from it?

Veronica said, saving him from more of the tough questions he didn't want to answer, "I've seen other Amish guys around the village, so I know how you wear your hair. I can cut it that way if you prefer."

"I'm not part of the Harmony Creek community."

"Oh, I assumed... That is, you're with Sarah, so I... Never mind." She kept her face averted as she reached for a pair of scissors on the narrow counter beneath the mirror.

Veronica thought he and Sarah were together? He couldn't ignore how his pulse quickened whenever he saw Sarah, but linking their names unsettled him. It was as if a thick vine wrapped around him, slowly tightening.

Natalie rushed over. "Can I have a blue streak in my hair?" She held up a magazine with a picture of a woman in her twenties who had blond hair except for a coil pinned behind her ear. It was as bright a blue as a roofing tarp.

"Why would you want to do that?" Sarah asked.

He was curious, too, why the little girl would want to do such a thing. Natalie's black hair would have to be bleached before the dye was applied.

"All the girls at school said they were going to do that this summer, and…"

She smiled. "Your *mamm* will be home before school starts. If she says it's okay, then I'll bring you back to have it done."

Natalie nodded. Maybe the girl had learned whining wasn't the way to persuade Sarah to change her mind. Or perhaps she really didn't want to dye her hair and was glad for an excuse not to.

Mia tugged on Sarah's apron. "If Natalie gets a blue streak, can I?"

"That's up to your *mamm*," Sarah replied in the same serene voice.

Alexander jammed his hands into his jean pockets as he walked to a chair on the other side of Toby. "She doesn't care what we do as long as we stay off the furniture." Bitterness tainted the boy's words.

Toby put a hand on the boy's shoulder. "*Mamms* and furniture." He captured the boy's gaze so Alexander couldn't miss how Toby rolled his eyes. "They don't understand a guy needs to put up his feet and chill now and then, ain't so?"

The boy cracked a smile, then chuckled. "You get yelled at about furniture, too?"

"Every guy has been told the same thing since Eve warned Cain and Abel to keep their feet off the sheepskin. Always the same things." Seeing how the *kinder* were listening with unusual intensity, he knew he couldn't stop now. He hoped the other adults understood he wanted to ease the boy's unhappiness. "We're always being told not to put our feet on the furniture. Wipe them off before we come in. Wash your hands and your neck. Don't forget to clean behind your ears. Do you think they go to school to learn how to nag at a guy?"

Alexander giggled along with the other *kinder*.

Behind Toby, Veronica laughed. "I like that one about Eve scolding her boys. I'll have to share it with my hubby. I can just hear him using it in a sermon some Sunday."

Her words seemed to be an invitation for each person in the salon to try to be silly. Even the old woman having her nails done pitched in with an absurd comment.

Toby let Veronica clip his hair while he listened. When he looked at the mirror, he saw Sarah regarding him with a smile. He gave her a wink, and color blossomed on her face. She turned away, and his smile broadened. He hadn't expected to have so much fun getting his hair cut.

By the time the buggy pulled into the farm lane and parked by the house she shared with her two brothers, Sarah's ears had been battered by dozens of questions from the *kinder*. They were beside themselves with curiosity about the trip she'd told them would include visits to two farms. If Toby, who sat beside her in the buggy's front seat, wondered where they were going, he didn't ask.

Maybe because he couldn't have gotten a word in edgewise. His repeated attempts to remind the *kinder* they needed to give Sarah a chance to answer one question before they asked another had been ignored.

She knew the big white farmhouse looked shabby next to the elegant house where the Summerhays family lived, but it now felt like home. The flowers she'd planted beside the front porch steps were flourishing, and the vegetable garden was lush with vegetables. She spent every Saturday and most evenings canning them so she and her brothers would have delicious vegetables in the depths of winter.

"Here we are." She shouted to be heard above the roar of the sawmill on the hill beyond the barn.

"What's that noise?" Natalie asked as she helped Mia and Ethan out of the buggy. All four *kinder* wore denim shorts and T-shirts along with sneakers.

"My brothers are sawing lumber."

"Why?" Mia put her hands over her ears. "It's loud."

"They're cutting lumber so people can use the wood to build things. Like buildings or furniture."

"Like wood?" asked the little girl.

"Lumber is wood." She smiled, astonished how much these *kinder* who'd been raised in the city needed to learn about country life, though they'd lived on the fancy estate for two years.

She had to wait until she could speak with Mr. Summerhays, but she hoped the *kinder's daed* would agree to letting them play with Amish *kinder*. It was important the kids get to know each other as individuals, not as plain or *Englisch*.

"So you grow wood here?" Mia was having a difficult time figuring it out.

"We have a wood lot." She smiled. "And, of course, a Christmas tree farm."

"Christmas tree farm?" Now it was Ethan's turn to look puzzled. "Don't Christmas trees come from the store?"

"*Real* trees are grown just like all the other plants God created for our world." She took the little boy's hand and held her other one out to Mia. "These aren't the artificial ones made out of plastic."

"We have a pink tree and a white one." Natalie grimaced. "Neither of them grew on a farm."

"We have plain old green ones. Would you like to see them?"

The four *kinder* nodded, even Alexander, who sometimes liked to pretend he wasn't interested in what his siblings were.

Sarah kept the pace slow enough so Toby could keep up with them. With the trees set into a hillside, the path rose steadily. Years of dragging cut trees had worn a gentle path between the rows.

The shriek of the saw ruined the quiet among the trees. Each time it halted, there was a moment of silence, and then the birds seemed to find their voices again. As the *kinder* looked around in awe at the trimmed Scotch pine and fir trees, their eyes seemed to get bigger and bigger.

Toby came to stand beside Sarah as she urged the youngsters to wander among the trees. When he added a warning to be careful and not damage them, she chuckled.

"I don't know what they could do to damage a Christmas tree," she said.

"Mrs. Hancock mentioned yesterday how, while you were helping me with my physical therapy, she found the boys fishing in their *daed's* tropical fish tank by tying strings onto chopsticks. After hearing that, I'm assuming they can always find something to create havoc."

Again, she laughed. "You're right."

Mia ran to them. "Why are there branches on the ground? Are the trees broken?"

Hearing the dismay in the *kind's* voice, Sarah knelt so she could look the little one in the eyes. "No, they aren't broken. We call those boughs."

"Like 'deck the halls with boughs of holly,'" said Ethan.

Mia bristled at her brother's superior tone. "These aren't holly! They're Christmas trees! What do we do with these?"

"Alexander, will you get the bags I put on the rear platform of the buggy? Let's gather the boughs, and I'll take you to visit someone who will know what to do with them."

Though the *kinder* tried to get her to explain further—and Toby asked a couple of times what she planned—Sarah would only say that they'd be happy they'd collected the boughs. She went to help the smaller two carry the boughs to where Toby held large plastic bags open.

He proved to be an excellent manager. He kept the four *kinder* running to collect the boughs that Benjamin had clipped off the trees before they arrived. The bags at the back of the buggy quickly filled.

As he teased the youngsters, making them laugh, Sarah felt her heart melt in the warmth of his smile. He was so *gut* with them, bringing out a silliness she'd never realized was there. He was luring her to be as zany, and it was *wunderbaar* to toss aside her worries about the future and revel in the day they were sharing.

Natalie held boughs to her face. "This smells cool."

"Hmm…" Toby bent to take a sniff. "To me, it smells warm. Like a fire in a fireplace. Like the scent of gingerbread."

"I meant cool as in…as in really…" She looked at Sarah for help.

"As in fabulous?" Sarah asked.

"*That's* what I meant."

Toby dropped the boughs into a bag. "I agree. The

scent is cool and warm at the same time." He glanced down when Mia tugged on his shirt. "Do you have something to add, munchkin?"

"You're goofy," she announced with the certainty of a four-year-old.

"Me?"

At his feigned shock, Sarah couldn't keep from laughing. The *kinder* joined in, but not Toby. He smiled.

She told herself she should be satisfied with seeing an honest smile on his face instead of the strained, false one he'd worn when he first arrived. She couldn't help wondering what his laugh sounded like. Would it resonate as his voice did?

Lord, You know the state of Toby's heart. He has allowed a bit of joy to enter it. Please help him keep it open for more happiness to sweep in.

What could she do to help? Getting an idea, she smiled and gathered the *kinder* near.

"Shall we pick out a tree now for you at Christmas?" she asked.

The excited youngsters cheered. Before they could scatter, she reminded them it was a decision they needed to make together.

For the next fifteen minutes, they wandered among the rows of trees. Once or twice, she thought the *kinder* might agree on one, but then another caught their eyes. She had to veto some because even the high ceilings in their house wouldn't accommodate such a towering tree.

"I like this tree." Ethan pointed to one not much taller than he was.

"Don't you think we should let it have a chance to grow a couple more years?" Sarah asked.

"If we get a bigger tree, then what if Daddy isn't home to put the star on top? *I* can put a star on top of this one."

Pretending she hadn't heard Toby's sharp intake of breath, Sarah knelt in front of the little boy. She blinked away her tears before they could escape and upset the *kind* more. Not just Ethan, but his siblings, who also looked ready to cry.

"Don't you like having a bigger tree better, Ethan?" she asked as she cupped his elbows to make a connection between them.

He nodded, his lips beginning to quiver. "It needs a star on top."

"I'll talk to your *daed* about the star."

"Daddy is busy."

"*Ja*, I know. We're months away from Christmas. We can figure something out between now and when the tree arrives at your house."

He wiped his nose against his sleeve. "Okay."

When she urged Ethan to join his siblings, who were discussing the merits of a nearby tree as if it were the most important decision ever made, she waited until he was out of earshot before she released the sigh that weighed on her heart.

Behind her, Toby said, "You surprised me, Sarah."

"How so?" She faced him.

"You're always working for those kids to challenge themselves. I thought you'd offer to help him put the star on the tree himself."

"I would have if he was worried about the star." She lowered her voice as she stepped closer to him. "What he really wants is time with his *daed*." Looking at the youngsters encircling a pretty Scotch pine, she added, "Just as Alexander was when he complained about his *mamm* being more worried about the furniture. *Danki* for drawing him out of his bad mood then."

"He was feeling sorry for himself."

"No, he wasn't. He isn't wrong, you know." She sighed. "His *mamm* spends a lot of time worrying about the furniture. I'm not sure why she changes it all the time. Whatever the reason, it keeps her away so often, and the *kinder* miss her. Those four *kinder* want someone—anyone—to pay attention to them."

"You said they want their parents' attention."

She put a hand on his arm to stop him from following the *kinder* up the hill. When he turned toward her, she said, "Of course they want their parents' attention first and foremost, but they'd be happy to have anyone's. That's why I try to take them places where they can be pampered a bit, like getting their hair cut or to the ice-cream shop."

"Have you mentioned this to them?"

"The *kinder*?"

He shook his head. "No, their parents."

"No."

"Why not?"

She clasped her hands behind her so he couldn't see how they tightened at the futility of the situation. "I don't want them to think I'm sticking my nose in where it doesn't belong. I'm their nanny, not a family member."

"Don't tell the *kinder* that. They treat you like a beloved *aenti*."

"Maybe, but an *aenti* isn't a *mamm*."

"Are you arguing for telling your bosses the truth or against it?" He gave her a taut smile. "As I've told you before, they're not going to fire you. Why would they when they've had so much trouble finding a nanny who will stay?"

"You're looking at this logically, and logic might not have anything to do with their reaction. If they do fire

me, then the *kinder* will have nobody other than a parade
of other caretakers."

"As they did before you were hired?"

"Ja."

She must choose the time to confront them, so they
would listen. How she wished Toby understood! He
wasn't going to remain in Harmony Creek Hollow to
see the consequences, so she had to trust her instincts.

Could she trust her instincts right now when her heart
begged to be given to him?

Chapter Ten

Toby recognized the name on the mailbox as Sarah turned the buggy into the lane leading to a farm set on a broad lawn. Wagler was the surname of her twin friends. He wondered which one they were visiting after collecting the pine boughs. Or would both women be there?

He thought about what he'd witnessed after church when Sarah and her three *gut* friends laughed and chatted together with an ease that suggested they'd known each other their whole lives. However, he'd discovered that they'd met only a few months ago.

Was it possible for him to build strong friendships as Sarah had? He'd avoided them, even while working on J.J.'s ranch. Maybe he should consider lowering his guard and explore the possibilities of developing more than work relationships. Friendships and—he glanced toward Sarah, who was focused on driving along the twisting lane—perhaps something more.

Then what? demanded the voice that always warned him away from making rash decisions.

He wanted to retort to the voice but had never won an argument with it in the past. The one time he'd refused to heed it when he was twelve ended with his heart being broken into uncountable pieces. Once burned, twice the fool to try again.

To ignore his thoughts, Toby looked at the farm ahead of them. It looked like the others they'd passed on their way along the twisting road into the hollow. There was a rambling white house, recently painted because it glistened in the sunshine. A broad yard was edged by flowerbeds and a vegetable garden. Every row seemed to be exploding with vegetables waiting to be picked.

Behind the house were three barns, a chicken coop and what looked like a rabbit hutch. A pen was filled with goats in every combination of white, black and brown. One barn was much larger than the others, and he guessed it held the farm's milking parlor. The rumble from the smallest outbuilding told him the Waglers had a diesel generator to run their milking lines and the air compressors that powered other equipment.

Toby listened to the excited *kinder* behind them as Sarah slowed the buggy beside the house. The youngsters scurried out as soon as the wheels stopped moving, but halted when Sarah asked them to wait in case he needed help.

He could get out of the buggy on his own but didn't gainsay her, knowing she was using him as an excuse to keep the youngsters from scattering like windblown leaves.

Alexander stepped up, flexed his muscles with a big grin and offered to help Toby. With one hand on the boy's scrawny shoulder, Toby made sure he didn't put too much weight on Alexander.

Doing so made it more awkward to get out than on his own. He grimaced as he shifted his balance onto his right side while trying not to knock the boy over. Gripping the edge of the windshield, he nodded his thanks to

Alexander, who was grinning as if he'd been the greatest help imaginable.

"*Danki*, Alexander," Sarah added, stepping toward them and steering the boy away without appearing to do so.

"Why are we here?" asked Natalie.

"You'll see."

"Why won't you tell us?" Ethan stuck out his bottom lip.

Sarah smiled and tapped it, making the boy grin and his siblings giggle. No wonder Sarah was so *gut* with Bay Boy. She'd shown the horse the same patience she exhibited with four impatient *kinder*. Not that she was passive. Quite to the contrary, because he'd seen her eyes filled with heated sparks, but she knew how to pick her battles and when.

When she hadn't said anything to him on the short trip from her brothers' farm, Toby was sure something was bothering her. He thought through their conversation among her family's Christmas trees. She'd been distressed by how Summerhays and his wife paid too little attention to their *kinder*, but she'd been ready to speak her mind on that subject.

So what was bothering her now?

You.

Again, the small voice in his mind startled him. He'd heard it as clearly as he could the birds chirping overhead and, for once, it wasn't warning him away from becoming too close to someone. Instead, it was telling him the reason why there might be a wall between him and Sarah.

Maybe it was for the best. Every day he lingered was another drawing him into the community in the hollow. Each moment he spent with Sarah enticed him to look forward to the next time they could be together. In spite of his determination, his life was being linked to hers and her neighbors.

That would change once J.J.'s trailer pulled into the long driveway of Summerhays Stables.

A door to the house opened, and a petite brunette walked toward them. He wasn't sure which twin she was until Sarah greeted her.

"Leanna, in case you don't remember, this is Toby Christner." Sarah smiled.

"Nice to see you again, Toby." The brunette who was shorter than Sarah turned to the *kinder*. "Now, let me see if I can match the right name to the right person." She pointed to each *kind* and spoke his or her name.

"How do you know I'm Mia?" asked the littler girl.

"Because Sarah told me you loved animals, and I can see how eager you are to meet my goats." Leanna held out her hand.

Without hesitation, Mia grasped it. The two led the way toward the pen where the goats rushed forward as Leanna approached. The little girl didn't falter when the animals, which must have seemed huge to her, crowded around the fence. A pure white kid jumped onto a plastic box so it could look at Mia.

"Will it bite?" the little girl asked.

"Any animal with teeth can bite." Leanna's voice was calm. "Snowball is a *gut* little girl and likes to have her head scratched between her horn buds."

Mia reached through the fence and touched the kid on the head. When her hand was butted, she giggled before scratching Snowball. She grinned at her siblings as more young kids pushed forward to get attention.

When Leanna opened the gate, Mia was the first to follow her into the pen.

"She's brave," Toby said.

"*Ja*, she is." Sarah's smile softened. "She adores animals, but it's more than that." She gestured toward where the *kinder* were now encircled by the goats. "They're hungry for love."

"The goats?"

"No, the *kinder*." She faced him. For a moment, sunshine glinted off her glasses, hiding the expression in her eyes. "They've been left behind too often."

"You're worried they're going to be hurt when I go back to Texas."

"Ja."

He wanted to ask how she would feel when he left, but he'd hurt his ankle, not his head, so he didn't have an excuse to ask a stupid question. Better to focus, as she was, on the youngsters.

"If you want," he said, "I'll wait here."

Shock filled her eyes. "No, that's not what I want. I don't know what I want." She grimaced. "Don't change what you're doing. The *kinder* will be upset when you go, but won't it be better to give them nice memories of your times together to enjoy when they think about you after you've left?"

Without giving him a chance to answer, she pointed at the buggy and asked him to bring a bag of pine boughs to the goats' enclosure. She lifted two bags off and walked toward the gate.

He sighed as she strode away. Nice memories of times together? Maybe that would be sufficient for the *kinder*, but he doubted it would be enough for him. Was it possible he'd been wrong? Could it be that time spent building a relationship had nothing to do with the pain of breaking that connection with someone? He wasn't sure any longer.

The pine boughs were a huge success for the goats who ate them as fast as the *kinder* could take them out of the bag. Sarah stood between Mia and Natalie as they hand-fed the goats. Leanna kept an eye on the boys and made sure no animal got too aggressive.

Sarah giggled when the goats tried to climb one another for the treat. If Mia made sure Snowball got more than her share, nobody said anything. Each Summerhays *kind* seemed to have a favorite or two among the small herd.

There were complaints from both the *kinder* and the kids when the bag was empty. Leanna was adamant that too much of a *gut* thing was bad for goats.

"How can fresh greens be bad for them when they eat tin cans?" asked Alexander, digging out a final bough from the bag.

"They don't eat cans," Leanna said as she rolled the plastic bag and held it too high for the goats to reach. "They will eat the paper stuck to the outside of cans, but not the metal itself. That's a *narrisch* story."

"What?"

"A crazy story," Sarah explained. "*Narrisch* means crazy. Or you can say someone is *ab in kopp*."

"*Kopp* means head, ain't so?" asked Ethan.

Sarah nodded. "I didn't realize you knew that."

"I want to learn to speak Amish so I can play with the kids in the hollow." He grimaced. "Not these kids, but the others."

"I know what you mean." She brushed dirt from an overeager goat's hooves off his back. "I didn't realize you knew the *kinder* here."

"I don't. Not yet." He turned to where Toby was leaning on the fence, his arms folded on the top. "Toby said we could have fun with them and go sledding after it snows."

"Did he?" She wondered when Toby had mentioned such things to them. Probably while they were collecting the boughs. Once she had a chance to speak to Mr. Summerhays, she wanted to introduce her charges to the local plain *kinder*. She had some ideas of how to do that, but she must make sure their *daed* approved.

As Ethan babbled about finding the biggest hill and riding on the fastest sled, she extracted the four youngsters from the herd. The goats stepped aside reluctantly. The *kinder* went out, telling Toby about everything they'd done, though he'd witnessed each minute. They skipped to the buggy to bring the other bags of pine boughs to the barn.

When Leanna closed the gate, she paused and looked at the goats feasting on the pine needles that had fallen on the ground.

Sarah waited beside her friend as the *kinder* followed Toby to the buggy. She couldn't keep from smiling. There was something so endearing about the strong but injured man listening to four youngsters vying to get his attention and asking his opinion. It would have been wiser to keep distance between him and the *kinder*—and her—but it was impossible.

"Be careful," Leanna said in not much more than a whisper as she latched the gate. "Don't get your hopes up, Sarah."

"My hopes up? On what?"

"On persuading Toby to stay here in our settlement."

"I'm not trying to convince him to stay in Harmony Creek Hollow." *I don't know if I want to stay.*

Leanna patted the head of a goat that butted her through the fence, looking for another treat. "It looks like you are. I'm not the only one who thinks so."

"Annie—"

"It's not just us. Lyndon asked me about you and Toby and your plans. Several people mentioned it to him after you arranged for Toby to check out the horses Mercy wants for her camp."

Lyndon was older than the twins. He lived nearby with his family, including his son, who was a *kind* Sarah had in mind for Alexander to play with. Now she wondered what the reaction would be if she asked.

"Your brother shouldn't listen to gossip or repeat it." Sarah struggled to swallow her dismay.

If her brothers heard such rumors and believed them, what would they do? They seemed determined to prevent her from making mistakes. They could insist she avoid Toby, though she had no idea how she would while working at the house where he lived.

Don't borrow trouble, her common sense warned her.

Leanna put kind fingers on Sarah's arm, and Sarah knew her thoughts had seeped out to be displayed on her face. "Don't worry, Sarah. Lyndon didn't speak about it to anyone but me. He wanted to know if it was true you and Toby were walking out together, because he planned to squelch the rumor if it wasn't."

"So you told him it wasn't so."

"I told him the truth. I didn't know if you were trying to convince Toby to stay or not." She wiped her hands on her apron.

"Toby has made it clear right from the beginning that as soon as his boss returns, he'll go home to Texas."

"Things change."

"Not that much. Toby loves his life in Texas."

"How much do you love your life in Harmony Creek Hollow?" Leanna looked away as she asked, "Would you leave here to go with him?"

"I've never given that idea the slightest thought." Whether she stayed plain or became *Englisch*, she intended to remain close to her family. Her brothers might want nothing to do with her, but she couldn't imagine walking away from them forever.

Leanna smiled. "I'm glad to hear that. You've become a dear friend, Sarah, and I wouldn't want you to leave the Harmony Creek Spinsters' Club."

A gasp came from behind her. Sarah whirled to see Toby standing there. How much of their conversation had he heard?

"Harmony Creek Spinsters' Club?" he repeated as his eyes widened. "Did I hear you right?"

"It's a joke." She hoped her face wasn't turning red, but the familiar heat warned her that her skin was becoming the same shade as her hair. "It's a name we older unmarried women gave ourselves when we decided to do more things together. We didn't want to call ourselves the 'Older Girls Club' because that sounds worse."

"But Harmony Creek *Spinsters'* Club?" He started to add more, but his words dissolved into a laugh that burst from deep within him.

She couldn't help but stare. There was such candid and unabashed joy in his eyes and his stance as he leaned on his crutches. The Summerhays *kinder* rushed over to discover what was behind his unexpected laughter.

Then she began to laugh, too. She hadn't imagined Toby's laughter, once freed, would be so infectious. When Leanna and the youngsters joined in, the goats began to bleat as if they wanted to be part of the merriment.

"Everyone tell Leanna *danki* for letting us visit her and her goats," Sarah said when she could talk again.

The chorus of responses included Toby's much deeper voice.

"*Komm* anytime," Leanna said. "I can always use helpers to feed the goats."

"Now," Sarah added to curtail pleas to stay longer, "we need to get home for lunch, lessons and—" she turned to Toby and said with a mock frown and a stern tone "—physical therapy."

The *kinder* and Toby gave emoted groans but went to the buggy. Sarah gave her friend a quick hug before following. They waved goodbye to Leanna as Sarah drove them toward the road that followed the sinuous Harmony Creek.

Again, the conversation in the back seat was non-stop until the youngsters scrambled out in front of the Summerhays house. They rushed up the porch steps, and Sarah reminded them they needed to wash first.

Toby followed her as she unhitched Charmer and put him to graze.

"I owe you an apology," he said.

"For laughing at our club's name?" Her grin ruined her attempt to sound serious.

"No, for mentioning about the kids going sledding with the other *kinder* without saying anything to you first. I don't know if I've stepped on your toes."

"You haven't. I've been thinking about ways to get the Summerhays *kinder* and the plain ones together to play when they're not in school. There aren't a lot of *Englisch kinder* nearby, and they need to have friends beyond each other."

"The *kinder* will be excited to have you act as a conduit for them to meet others their own ages among the *Leit*."

"I grew up with a group of five other girls who were with me from diapers to school and beyond. We did everything together, learning to cook and do farm chores and take care of the smaller ones. We helped each other in school and, when we were old enough, we attended singings and other youth gatherings together. I know how important those friendships have been to me."

"Do you still hear from them?" he asked as they walked toward the kitchen door.

"*Ja*. We have a circle letter that was started when the first of us moved away. Now we live in three states and five districts."

"You've got a miniature version of *The Budget*, ain't so?"

She laughed at the comparison. "The circle letter keeps us up-to-date on what the rest of the family is doing. Between the six of us cousins, we connect to two hundred people."

"You and your friends are cousins?"

"*Ja*. My *daed* had seven brothers and six sisters."

"And your *mamm*?"

"Was an only *kind*." She laughed at the memory of *Mamm* telling how much trouble she had learning all her future in-laws' names.

"As I was."

She stopped to pick up an early hazelnut that had fallen in the yard. Its husk tried to stick to her fingers, but she rolled it along her palm. "I can't imagine that." She tossed the nut into the bushes for a squirrel to find. "Or maybe I can because it's just Benjamin, Menno and me now. I miss the rest of the family. Do you miss yours?"

"Not really. After our first move, we never lived near family again."

"My brothers may be overbearing at times, but they're family." She paused as they reached the back door. "I'm sorry you missed out on having a chance to get to know your extended family."

"I am, too." His eyes widened. "Usually when people say things like that, I shrug it off. However, you're right.

After seeing what the Summerhays kids share, it makes me wish I could have had that, too."

"You can have it now. Either with the kids, who think of you as a big brother, or in our community."

"You know I'm only staying until I get the *doktor's* okay to work, ain't so?"

"Of course, but why not enjoy what's here while you do?" She wasn't sure if she'd have another chance to share these thoughts with him. Having the *kinder* with them most of the day, it wasn't simple to discuss serious issues. "Natalie loves talking about horses with you."

"Ja."

"Alexander and Ethan need a man to talk to. I can help the girls with things unique to girls, but with the boys, it's not as easy." She smiled. "You were a boy. You know how they think and feel. Would you—while you're here recovering—be that person they can turn to?"

"I'll have to think about it. Being a mentor to a *kind* is a big responsibility, Sarah."

"The biggest, but from what I've seen of you, you aren't a man who avoids responsibility. If you were, you wouldn't be miserable waiting to get back on a horse and continue training those three horses you brought from Texas."

"And spending a day at the stables in Saratoga."

Her smile returned. "Don't worry. I haven't forgotten. If you get the okay from the *doktor*, I'll talk to Mr. Summerhays about taking you there."

"In the meantime, I'll come up with ways to spend more time with the boys."

"Danki," she said.

His gaze swept her face and held her eyes. His eyes narrowed ever so slightly as his fingers curved along her cheek. Startled by her powerful reaction to his questing touch, she recoiled. He lifted his hand away, but she edged toward him again.

He murmured her name. Or she thought he did. Her heart was thumping too hard for her to hear anything as his fingers cupped her chin. As he tilted her face toward his, she held her breath, wondering if his kiss would be as sweet as she hoped.

When his lips brushed her cheek, she bit her lower lip to keep her sigh of disappointment from escaping. She blinked as he opened the door to release the cacophony of four *kinder* talking at once. His "*danki*" remained behind when he entered, leaving her outside alone.

She turned away and wrapped her arms around herself, cold though the day remained hot and humid. How *narrisch* she'd been to think he'd kiss her! He'd been honest from the beginning. He couldn't wait to leave for his life with its few obligations. He knew how he wanted his life to go. She'd been *dumm* to think anything—or anyone—could change that.

Especially Sarah Kuhns.

Chapter Eleven

Sarah's brothers were quiet the next evening during supper. Instead of discussing, as they usually did, their day at the sawmill and what they would do the next morning, Menno and Benjamin were as silent as the clock she'd forgotten to wind before she left for the Summerhays house. They spoke only when they asked for food to be passed. As always, the evening meal was smaller than the midday meal. She'd prepared a casserole with ham leftover from earlier in the week along with cheese and pasta. A salad with vegetables she'd picked an hour ago in the garden and the bread she'd baked yesterday shared the table with pickles and apple butter and a bowl of chowchow.

Each attempt she made at starting a conversation failed while her brothers ate. Even when she asked how much longer it would take to fill the corncrib, they shrugged at the same time. That startled her because any other night, they would have given her a lecture about how, as a woman, she didn't need to worry about the crops and that she should focus her concerns on her garden and the house.

She tightened her grip on her fork before setting it on her plate. Miriam and the Wagler twins didn't have to endure such reprimands. Their families treated them like vital members, not a fragile piece of china that needed to be guarded from encountering the realities of life on a farm.

When they had first moved to the hollow along Harmony Creek, she'd assumed her brothers' reluctance to be honest with her was because of their fears they couldn't make the farm a success. They'd set up the sawmill, tilled the fields and planted apple trees. It would take three years before the trees bore fruit, but in the meantime, Menno and Benjamin could build their other businesses.

However, her brothers were determined to farm. It'd been three generations since the Kuhns family had depended on fields for their livelihood. What once had been their farm in Indiana had been sold acre by acre until only a single one remained. The men had worked in the RV factories or in shops owned by *Englischers*.

Their first harvest was about to get underway, and they were concerned about the amount of corn they expected to get from the few arable fields attached to their farm. The old corncrib had been emptied and swept out. Slats to prevent animals from getting in had been replaced. She guessed the corn, when stripped from the stalks, would fill about half of it.

"More biscuits?" she asked, holding up the plate.

Benjamin took two and mumbled a "*danki*," but Menno didn't glance in her direction.

Her brothers couldn't look less alike. Menno had hair as dark as a bear's. In fact, his friends in Indiana had called him Big Brother Bear before he was baptized. Benjamin's hair had red highlights but was otherwise a plain brown. Both men had work-worn hands with layers of calluses from the long hours they'd spent at the sawmill or in the fields. Though neither brother would admit it, she guessed they'd discovered they didn't like farming as much as they'd hoped. As soon as they could make a go with the sawmill, she suspected the fields would be rented to a neighbor. Most likely to David Bowman, because she'd heard her brothers discuss having sheep near their house.

After a second silent prayer of thanks when their dessert of chocolate cake with maple frosting was gone, Sarah began to clear the table. She set the dishes in the sink and ran hot water. The dish detergent spit air, and she knew she needed to add another bottle to her shopping list for the next time she went into Salem to grocery shop with her friends. She turned to write it on the whiteboard hanging on the refrigerator.

"Sit for a minute," Menno said before she could return to the sink. "We need to talk."

"About what?" she asked as she wiped her hands on the dish towel. Hanging it on the oven door's handle, she walked to the table.

Her brothers exchanged glances but remained silent while she pulled out her chair and sat.

She was tempted to tell them they'd explained everything to her with that single shared look. How many times had she seen it since *Daed* died and her brothers took his place as head of their household? More times than she cared to count.

Each time, she saw those expressions before they were ready to announce something she wasn't going to like. They hadn't liked the idea of her working out as a nanny. They weren't sure she should spend so much time with her friends in the Harmony Creek Spinsters' Club. *Ach*, she was grateful she hadn't mentioned that name in front of them!

Worst of all was the look they aimed at each other—

and at her—when she'd talked about becoming an EMT. They'd acted as if she'd announced she wanted to run off and join a Broadway show. Her brothers had refused to discuss it, even Benjamin, who could be more reasonable. They were so certain of their decision that they seemed to believe she was the one who couldn't see the truth.

Sarah folded her hands on her lap and waited to discover what her brothers had to say.

As always, Menno, as the oldest, took the lead. "Our sawmill is doing better with each passing week. We're gaining more customers. Many are our neighbors, who are fixing farmhouses in the hollow, but others are *Englischers* who wish to have custom work done for their homes or businesses."

"That's *gut*," she said with a sincere smile. "You've worked hard to establish the sawmill as the go-to place for fresh lumber."

"Go-to?" asked Benjamin.

"Something the Summerhays *kinder* say. It means—"

Menno interrupted her. "We know what it means. I didn't know you did."

"I hear the same things you do."

"I'm sure you hear more at that *Englisch* house."

She frowned. "Why are you acting distressed about my job? I've been there since the end of last year. You've been grateful for my wages and how I have time to take care of this house as well as be a nanny for the *kinder*."

"Things change." Menno raised his chin as if daring her to contest his statement.

"I agree." She wasn't going to quarrel with her brothers.

Benjamin surprised her when he said, "Get to the point, Menno." He usually went along with whatever their older brother did.

When Menno refused to meet her eyes, she could

contain her curiosity no longer. "*Ja*, Menno," she said, "please say what you want to talk to me about. I'd like to get the dishes done in time to do mending before bed."

Menno drew in a deep breath, then said in a rush, "James Streicher is interested in meeting you."

She searched her mind. Three families had moved into the settlement along Harmony Creek in the past month, but she couldn't recall anyone by that name. There had been a tall, thin man she didn't recognize at the last church Sunday services. Was he James Streicher?

"I don't think I know him," she said.

Her brothers looked at each other again before turning to her.

Benjamin answered this time. "We met him yesterday. He's sharing a house with the Frey family while he builds his own place next door."

"Next door to the Freys?" She thought the Troyers lived there.

"No, next door to us." He pointed to the east.

"There's another farm between us and the Freys?"

"Not a farm. Just a couple of acres on the other side of the creek, but James doesn't need much space. He's a blacksmith. The last *Englisch* smith closed his forge a year or so ago. There's a real need for a blacksmith in the area."

She thought of Frank and the rumor he'd heard about a blacksmith coming to Harmony Creek. "It sounds as if James has seen a *gut* opportunity in our new settlement."

"James's got a *gut* head on his shoulders." That was the finest compliment Menno could give. He had no use for emotion, only common sense and hard work.

Which made Sarah wonder why he didn't offer her more respect. She worked hard every day at the Summerhays house while making a home for her brothers. When they had to stay late at the sawmill or while doing other chores around the farm, she never once complained. She kept their meals ready for them whenever they wanted to eat.

"He's come from Milverton in Ontario," Menno added. "In Canada."

Not wanting to tell him she knew geography, too, she replied in the same steady tone, "I don't think I've ever met anyone from those districts." She smiled at her brothers, wondering why they were making such a big deal about a new neighbor. "I'll make sure I greet James after our next church service and welcome him to our settlement."

"Make sure you talk to him," Menno said. "It'll be better if you do before he brings you home from the singing."

Sarah sat straighter, her eyes widening. She must have heard her brother wrong. He expected her to accept an invitation for a ride home with a stranger from a youth event that she hadn't planned to attend?

Impossible.

As she started to say that, Menno waved her to silence. "You didn't hear me wrong, Sarah. James will be bringing you home from the singing."

"You told him I'd let him do that? Without mentioning it to me first?"

"You've been running around with your friends long enough, Sarah. Benjamin and I agree it's time for you to marry. As your brothers, we want to see you settled."

"Whether or not I'm happy to be settled with someone I've never met is irrelevant, ain't so?"

"We don't want you to be miserable," Benjamin said, shooting a frantic look at their older brother.

"But," Menno continued, as if they'd practiced the conversation—and she wouldn't have been shocked to learn that they had, "if you're going to argue you need to fall in love first, you know many marriages have been successful though the couple weren't in love when they married."

"I didn't realize either of you was an expert on either love or marriage."

Sarah should have wanted to take back the words as soon as she spoke them because she saw how Benjamin cringed, but she was too angry. She'd heard whispers about Benjamin and a young woman walking out together in Indiana, but even if it'd been true, the young woman had married someone else.

Was her brother the victim of a broken heart? Had he waited too long as Leanna had to share the truth with the one he loved?

Her sympathy for Benjamin was swept aside when Menno stood and pointed at her. "You will agree to this, little sister. We know it's time for you to be done with your work as a nanny and for you to start a family of your own. James has seen you, and he's willing to walk out with you in spite of your bizarre ideas."

"Like learning to help others as an EMT?" She rose, too, though she knew she was throwing oil on the fire of her brother's fury.

"He knows—as I do…I mean, as *we* do—that a plain woman's place is taking care of her family, not *Englisch* ones."

"But—"

"I won't argue about it. Our minds are made up." Menno whirled on his heel and stamped away.

She looked at Benjamin. Again, he wouldn't meet her eyes as he stood and followed their older brother into the front room.

Frustration sent her toward the back door. This time,

her well-meaning brothers had gone way too far. She grabbed her bonnet off the peg and tied it beneath her chin. Going out, she prayed a walk would give her enough time to cool down.

She wondered if it was possible to walk that long.

Toby was standing by the pasture fence and watching Bay Boy go through his exercises with Mick, the most skilled groom at Summerhays Stables. Bay Boy wasn't as skittish with the other man as he'd been when Mick first started working with him. The horse was confused why Toby remained on the other side of the fence.

"Don't let him turn so slowly!" Toby called. "He needs to lean into the turn if he's going to keep up with the field."

Mick motioned he'd heard as he continued to work with the horse.

"He's stubborn, isn't he?" Natalie asked as she came to stand beside Toby.

He stared at the *kind* in astonishment. There wasn't an inch of her not covered with mud. Had she been rolling in puddles?

As if he'd asked aloud, she said, "We've been building a castle behind the house."

"Where they've been taking down the trees?"

Ethan bounded to join them. "It's the best, Toby! You need to come and see our castle." The boy and the other two who appeared on his heels were as filthy as Natalie.

"It looks as if you've been having a *gut* time," Toby said with a laugh. Odd how easily laughter came now that he no longer tried to dam it inside him.

He listened as they told him how they'd dug around the disturbed ground and how Alexander had the big idea to link the holes to form a moat. When they finished their tale, he sent them off to the stable to wash off before going into the house. He doubted Mrs. Hancock would appreciate four mud-covered youngsters on the fancy floors and carpets.

When they scurried away, Toby turned to watch Bay Boy finish his session. His eyes focused on a familiar form that appeared from among the trees at the far side of the pasture. Sarah was coming across the meadow. He waved to her and smiled when she changed direction to come toward where he stood.

His smile faded as she strode past him and inside the house. She hadn't acknowledged him.

Turning, he hobbled into the smaller living room with its large fieldstone fireplace and beamed ceiling. He ignored the fancy overstuffed furniture and elegant wooden tables, his gaze focused on Sarah. He was amazed she didn't pound her feet right through the floor. He jammed the crutches under his arms and moved so he was in her path as she turned to storm across the room.

She stared at him. "What are you doing, Toby?"

"Trying to make sure you don't wear out your shoes with pacing."

"Leave me alone." She pushed around him and kept going as if the answer to whatever she sought was ahead of her.

"If you wanted to be alone, then why are you here?"

She halted midstep and blinked several times without speaking. At last, she said, "I'm not sure."

"About why you're here?"

"That and everything else." She began walking again. "I was headed out for a walk in the woods, then I ended up here." She gestured toward the door. "The woods aren't too wide between this house and my brothers' farm."

"Sit down, Sarah. I can't keep up with you."

She sank into the closest chair.

He pulled another closer to where she sat. Resting his crutches against his chair, he slanted toward her, his clasped hands between his knees.

"Danki," he said.

"For what?"

"For not making me chase you in order to find out what's going on." He appraised the tight lines he'd never seen in her face before. Emotion exploded through him. Anger, he was shocked to discover. He'd been angry plenty of times, but not like this. It was a cold anger ready to be detonated at whomever had caused her to pull inside herself like an armadillo curled into an armored ball. "What's wrong?"

She didn't answer him right away. Instead, she stared at her hands in her lap. Her knuckles were colorless, warning she was clenching her hands to the point they must hurt.

He reached across the space between them and put his hand over hers. He wanted to pry her fingers apart as he banished whatever was upsetting her, but he forced himself to do nothing but gently stroke her soft skin.

"What's wrong?" he asked again in a whisper. "Will you tell me?"

Raising her eyes, she met his gaze. He could see the flood of tears she was holding in by sheer will. "My brothers."

"What about them?"

"They're playing matchmaker."

"For each other?"

A reluctant smile tipped her lips for the length of a single heartbeat. "If they were doing that, I wouldn't be upset. They're matchmaking for me."

He arched his brows. "Brothers setting up their sisters with fellows is a pretty common occurrence."

"You don't understand. They've matched me with James Streicher, a man I've never met."

"He's a newcomer to the settlement?"

"So new he doesn't have a home of his own yet."

"So they knew him when you lived in Indiana?"

She shook her head again. "He's from Canada. They met him for the first time yesterday."

"They want you to marry him after they've met him a single time?"

He hadn't had a chance to speak with her brothers yet, but if they had half as much integrity as Sarah, they must be honest, *gut* men. Making such a snap judgment about a stranger made no sense.

"That's what they said." She wrung her hands together again in her lap. "After being so overprotective of me that they make it hard for me to breathe, now they're ready to hand me off to someone I've never met."

"Are you going to do as they ask?"

Her head whipped up. "Menno is the head of our household. It behooves me to do as he asks."

"Behooves?" He was rewarded by her faint, swift smile, but it faded again. "That sounds like the Sarah Kuhns you don't want to be. The one who wouldn't help the kids because she's worried about her job."

"I don't want to be that person."

"I know that. You'd rather be the Sarah Kuhns who lets everyone know how she feels. The one who longs for something she doesn't know she can have if she's Amish."

Her eyes grew so round that he could see white around her deep brown irises. "I've never said anything about that."

"No, you haven't, but you've said a lot about making sure the Summerhays *kinder* have the lives they want."

"I have?"

"About them having time with their parents and asking me to help with the boys. You're trying to give them plenty of experiences so they can learn and do things they may not be able to imagine now." He took her hands and folded them between his. "You don't want them to feel smothered as you do by your brothers' *gut* intentions."

She sighed as she stood. "*Smothered* is the exact word."

He pushed himself to his feet, too. "So what are you going to do about it?" he asked as he had when they spoke of the *kinder's* longing to spend time with their parents.

Unlike that time, she didn't square her shoulders and give him a strong, assertive answer. Instead, she hung her head and whispered, "I don't know."

He could have no sooner stopped his arms from enfolding her to him than he could have stopped the sun from rising the next morning. As he drew her against his chest, she pressed her face to his heart. He wondered if she could hear how it was breaking.

For her, because she was torn between her hopes for the future and what her brothers had planned for her?

Or was it shattering for himself as he realized he would never have another chance to hold this woman who fit so perfectly in his arms?

Chapter Twelve

On the next Sunday morning, a humid day where breathing was so hard Toby could have believed he was underwater, he found it hard to accept that two weeks had passed since the last time he'd sat on the front steps and watched for a buggy. It meant he'd completed nearly half of his banishment to Summerhays Stables.

Banishment? It didn't feel like that any longer. He was able to go to the stables, though he had to remain on the sidelines so the crutches didn't spook the horses. Even so, he could watch as the three horses they'd brought from Texas, along with the others, were exercised. He spent time talking with the stablemen about the horses and their idiosyncrasies. He learned training for Summerhays's horses began at these stables, and only the horses that achieved a certain competency were taken to the stables in Saratoga for further training.

In addition to his physical therapy, he spent time with the Summerhays *kinder*. He watched them take their swimming lessons while he put his foot in the hot tub, letting the jets work on loosening the muscles. He enjoyed talking with Natalie, who knew more about horses than most grown-ups, including people he'd worked with on

J.J.'s ranch. He and Natalie had developed an easy rapport. She tried to stump him with questions and, so far, he'd been able to answer each one. The other kids would join them, but none was as horse-crazy as Natalie.

Then there was Sarah. Each morning as he opened his eyes, his first thought was how blessed he was to spend time with her. He hadn't had an excuse to hold her again as he had the evening she'd wandered from her home to the pasture out by the stable, seeking an answer to her dilemma. He doubted he'd done anything to help her make that decision simpler, but the memory of her, warm and soft, in his arms warned him his attempts to be standoffish with everyone until J.J. and Ned returned had been futile. He couldn't wait each day to see Sarah. Even last Sunday when there had been no church service, she'd come by to take him to visit with her neighbors.

They hadn't stopped at her family's farm, and she hadn't introduced him to her brothers. Toby didn't know if they wanted nothing to do with him or she was avoiding what might be an uncomfortable meeting. Though she hadn't said, he sensed she feared if her brothers discovered how much time she was spending with him, Menno and Benjamin would become more insistent she marry the new blacksmith.

He looked at his bound right ankle. The worst of the swelling had vanished, leaving a variety of colors from a plum purple to a banana yellow laced across his foot and on his shin. Gone, too, was the devastating pain of the first weeks. Each motion threatened to bring it back, but he'd learned to avoid movements that sent a jagged shard slicing along his leg.

Sarah had helped him get to this point. He must not do anything to make the situation worse for her.

Though he'd tried several times in the past three days

to turn their conversations to her brothers' matchmaking, she'd refused to speak of it. He wasn't sure if that was a *gut* thing or bad. One fact was irrefutable. She was going to remain in the Harmony Creek settlement, and he was heading to Texas as soon as J.J. got back.

A gray-topped buggy drove up the long drive toward the house. Toby came to his feet. Sarah had been quite clear her family wouldn't be trading their black Indiana buggy for a Lancaster County style one until after the harvest was in.

Who...?

The buggy stopped, and a short man with a thick brown beard stepped out. He reminded Toby of someone, but Toby wasn't sure whom.

"I'm Lyndon Wagler," said the man. "My sisters, Annie and Leanna, are friends with Sarah. When she mentioned you'd need a ride to the service, I volunteered."

"Danki," he said, glad he had to concentrate on getting himself and his crutches into the cramped buggy.

That way, neither Lyndon nor his wife and *kinder* could get a glimpse of his expression. Before he'd been able to control his face, he knew his disappointment must have been visible on it. Why hadn't Sarah mentioned to him that she was sending someone to collect him for the service?

His stomach ached as if Bay Boy had driven a hoof into it. Could she have gone on her date with the newcomer and taken such a liking to the man she wanted to avoid complications by being seen with Toby? She hadn't said when she was seeing James. Had Toby been wrong to assume it would be after the youth singing tonight? No, he realized. She had arranged for someone to get him so she didn't have to bring him home when she was supposed to ride with James tonight.

Everything made sense.

And everything made his stomach threaten to erupt.

Making sure he was wearing an innocuous smile as he sat in the front next to Lyndon, Toby turned to say, *"Gute mariye."*

Lyndon's wife, who introduced herself as Rhoda, smiled before cautioning her young son and daughter to stop trying to peer out the rear of the buggy. Chuckling, Lyndon added that too often they had to halt the buggy to collect hats or bonnets that had fallen off the *kinder's* heads when they tried to see everything they passed.

Toby appreciated the Waglers' easy acceptance of him as they drove to the Troyers' house at the end of the hollow. When they pulled to a stop before a big farmhouse that looked as if it'd had recent repairs to its roof, he wondered how many different homes he'd entered on church Sundays. He'd lost count years ago. At least on this church Sunday, many of the faces were familiar from when he'd worshipped with these people two weeks ago.

While Rhoda took her *kinder* and went to stand with the women, Toby and Lyndon joined the other men waiting to enter the house with the beginning of the service. Which one was James?

It was easy to pick out Sarah's brothers. The family resemblance was strong between the siblings. They must be a decade older than she was. Neither wore a beard, showing they hadn't married, which was surprising.

Maybe, like him, they hadn't felt at home in one place and didn't want to put down roots and make connections until they found that place where they intended to stay. No, that didn't make sense. As far as he knew, Sarah had lived in only one community near Goshen, Indiana, before moving to Harmony Creek. Unless her brothers had jumped from district to district as his parents had, they came to the hollow from northern Indiana, as well.

As if he called to them, the Kuhns brothers edged toward him through the gathering of men. Lyndon gave him a bolstering smile before going to talk to a tall man Toby knew was Caleb Hartz, the man who'd gathered the families together for the new settlement.

"I'm Menno Kuhns," said the man with the darker hair. "This is my brother, Benjamin."

"*Gut* to meet you. I'm—"

"We know who you are. Toby Christner, the Amish cowboy who's living with the Summerhays family out on the main road."

"I work with horses, not cows." He tapped one crutch with the other. "Though right now, I'm not doing much of either."

His attempt at levity was wasted. The Kuhns brothers continued to scowl at him as if he were a snake they'd found in the henhouse.

"You're from Texas, we hear." Benjamin spoke but kept glancing at his brother.

Toby was curious why. *"Ja."*

"You're here for only a short time?"

He hit one crutch with the other. "I'm here until I can get rid of these."

"Looks as if you're doing pretty *gut* now."

Toby felt his feigned smile wither, and he struggled to keep it in place. Even if Sarah hadn't confided in him about her brothers' plans to match her with someone she didn't know, he would have been able to gauge what the real meaning was behind the interrogation. The Kuhns brothers wanted to make sure he remembered he wasn't staying long in Harmony Creek Hollow.

Why didn't they just come out and ask how long he

was staying? He didn't appreciate their sly attempts to ferret out information he would have given them without a second thought. Did they think he would tell them a bold-faced lie? What sort of man did they think he was?

He flinched at the thought. Had the tales of his *daed's* troublemaking reached the brothers? His *daed* had believed he knew more than any minister or bishop, and he never hesitated to give his opinion, whether welcome or not. That outspokenness had vexed many people who hadn't liked the idea of a newcomer trying to change their ways. Corneal Christner had never learned, making the same mistakes as he moved his family from one district to another, always looking for those who would agree with his outrageous opinions.

Toby didn't remember living in northern Indiana, but families in one settlement had friends and family members in others, so rumors—both true and exaggerated— were shared along the Amish grapevine. Letters and gossip exchanged by neighbors moved more swiftly than the news printed in *The Budget*.

"I've been told it'll be a couple more weeks," he said coolly, "before I can head out of here."

The two men exchanged another glance before Benjamin said, "Sarah knows, ain't so?"

"She was there when I got the *gut* news. Your sister has been a blessing. She helps with my physical therapy. She has a real gift for helping those in need." He shouldn't have said the last, but he didn't like how the Kuhns brothers acted as if she couldn't form a single worthwhile thought on her own.

"Ja," Menno said in his grim tone. "She'll make a *gut mamm*, tending to scraped knees and other childish injuries. Anyone can see that."

"That's true."

"Soon enough, she'll be settled here," Menno added, reminding Toby of how his *daed* had made his comments in a tone that suggested no sane person would argue with them.

The rebellion and irritation inside him were familiar. How many times had Toby heard his *daed* say such things and then watched as others reacted? Too many to count. Each time, Toby had wanted to shout that his *daed* spoke for himself alone. There were those who deemed the son should suffer for the sins of his sire, but they seemed to forget that God had promised in the Old Testament to make sons suffer if their *daeds* hated God. Corneal Christner didn't hate God. He insisted that others share his ideas of how to worship Him and live in His service.

The Kuhns brothers walked away without another word. That told Toby—in no uncertain terms—even if he had two legs that worked as they were supposed to, he wouldn't be welcome if he went to see Sarah at her house. Her brothers didn't want her spending time with him.

If he pushed the issue, he feared Sarah would be the one to suffer. As he and his *mamm* had suffered, time and again, for his *daed's* insistence that he knew more than others. After seeing his *mamm's* grief each time they'd prepared to move again, he knew he couldn't be the cause of Sarah suffering the same sorrow.

James Streicher gave Sarah a faint smile as he held out a stack of plates covered with cupcake and cookie crumbs. The food had vanished during a break in the youth group's singing. She put the three plates she held on the others and thanked him. When he said he was glad to help, those were the first words he'd spoken to her. She waited for him to add something, but he turned on his heel and walked away.

Was he shy? If so, why had he agreed to her brothers' suggestion that he escort her home from the evening's events? Maybe he'd been too timid to ask her himself.

Her eyes were caught by an uneven motion by the door, and her heart leaped to attention. Her joy deflated when she realized it wasn't Toby, but a teen boy who'd broken his leg when he fell asleep and toppled off a wagon.

She'd hoped Toby would remain for the singing but guessed he'd left with the Waglers. Each church Sunday, Lyndon got his family home in time for him to do barn chores, so he would have left earlier in order to get Toby to Summerhays Stables.

She sighed when she saw the teens streaming out of the barn. They'd be pairing up for rides home in open courting buggies. It seemed like a lifetime ago she'd hoped Wilbur would ask her to go with him. Before she got to know him well, he'd seemed lighthearted compared to her brothers. How wrong she'd been!

When she couldn't remain behind in the barn any longer, she went outside. Most of the buggies had left. The few who weren't courting were clumped in groups of three or more to share the walk home along the dark, twisting road. Each group had at least one flashlight with them. *Englisch* drivers often sped or raced on the road, so it was vital to have something to show them pedestrians were there.

James stood by his buggy. Even in the fresh air, the odor of smoke and heated metal drifted from him. He helped her into the buggy, and she gave him a grateful smile. She wasn't sure if he saw it in the dim light from the Troyers' front porch. She waited for him to say something, but he was silent other than giving his horse the command to go.

He didn't speak while they drove along the road, taking care to avoid walkers.

Unable to endure the strained silence any longer, she said, "I appreciate you giving me a ride home."

"You live right next door to me, so it makes sense."

She smiled again, glad he'd given her more than a single-word reply. To keep the conversation going, she asked, "Do you like our new settlement?"

"I've been here only a few days, so I can't have an opinion yet. So far, so *gut*." There was a hesitation, then he asked as if realizing he needed to say more, "How about you? Do you like living along Harmony Creek?"

"I'm looking forward to seeing fall, because the *Englischers* I've spoken with tell me these hills and mountains are glorious when the trees begin to take on their autumn colors."

"Are you with the *Englisch* often?"

"I'm working as a nanny for an *Englisch* family out on the road to Rupert."

"That is *gut*. I'm sure your brothers appreciate your help when they have to focus on getting the sawmill going."

James drew in the buggy near one of the few *Englisch* homes along the road. The gaslight on top of an antique lamppost washed over them, allowing her to see his face. She averted hers because she wasn't sure what her expression might reveal.

"May I ask you a question?" he asked.

"Certainly." She forced herself to look from her folded hands to the man beside her.

"This whole me taking you home was your brothers' idea, ain't so?"

"They think it'd be a *gut* idea if we got to know each other better."

He smiled, shocking her because until then he'd been as serious as a sinner confessing before the *Leit*. "That's a nice way of saying I'm right. You're a nice person, Sarah."

"*Danki*. You've been kind to me, too."

"Kindness and attraction isn't the same thing."

"No."

A long sigh swept out of him. "I'm glad you agree, Sarah. I wouldn't want you to get the wrong impression."

"That you're desperate for a wife?"

"*Ja*." His smile returned. "As you're desperate for a husband."

"Is that what you think?" She halted herself from asking if others thought that way, too.

"Not at all, but your brothers suggested you were."

"They said that?" Sarah bit her lower lip to keep her annoyed words from escaping. She hadn't imagined her brothers would say such a thing to a stranger.

"If it makes you feel better, Sarah, I never believed a popular woman like you was desperate for a husband."

"*Danki*." She meant that sincerely. "And *danki* for being so nice about this."

"I've got older siblings, too, who think they know more than I do." He sighed. "I wouldn't say *ja* if someone asked me if I left Milverton because I was tired of their interference in my life, because one is supposed to speak well of one's family, but..."

"But?"

"I wouldn't want to lie, either, and say that person was wrong."

She relaxed, letting her shoulders ease from their stiff stance. "My brothers mean well, and I know they love me."

"As my older siblings do me. One saved me when I

was little from falling into the farm pond and drowning. However, once I was old enough to swim and look both ways along the road, they didn't believe anything had changed."

Sarah laughed, something she'd doubted she'd do while with him tonight. "Maybe your older siblings and mine are the same people. They act the same."

He chuckled with a rasp she guessed came from his hours in his smoky smithy. "That would explain a lot, ain't so?"

"I'm sorry Menno and Benjamin welcomed you to Harmony Creek Hollow like this."

"Don't be. I'm glad to have a chance to talk with you. I could use insight about the settlement." He laughed again. "From someone who isn't focused on having me marry his sister."

"Ask whatever you want."

Sarah was able to answer most of his questions about where to shop for groceries and how to advertise his services. Several of the men with businesses had hung flyers at the hardware store in Salem and found work that way. Word of mouth had taken over from there, and many of their *Englisch* neighbors looked for help from the plain artisans. When she mentioned Mr. Fleetwood was interested in selling his blacksmithing tools, James was thrilled to hear that.

"I'm going to have to thank your brothers," he said with a grin, "for insisting on me taking you home tonight. You've been a great help."

"Feel free to ask anyone for help. We're learning the best ways to live here. Any questions you've got, we've had at one time or another."

"That's *gut* to hear. Look, Sarah, I know your brothers are worried about someone named Toby. They mentioned several times they were unhappy about you getting involved with a drifter." He frowned. "Though, I have to say, from what I can see, you've got a *gut* head on your shoulders."

"Toby works at the same place I do. He was injured, so my boss asked me to help him with his physical therapy." The words were bitter on her lips, but they were the truth. Her foolish heart begged her to give it to him, but Toby had been honest with her from the beginning. He couldn't wait to leave for Texas.

"Maybe so, but your brothers are determined to keep you from walking out with him. And I don't have time for their matchmaking. I assume you don't, either."

"You're right."

"Here's what we can do. We'll talk to each other when we encounter each other, whether at Sunday services or during the week. That's what *gut* neighbors do anyhow."

"True."

"Being seen together should encourage your brothers— and anyone else interested—that we're aware of each other. Maybe more. We can leave that to their imaginations. In the meantime, your brothers will back off, and I can focus on getting my business going. Is that okay with you?"

"I wouldn't want to lie."

"I'm not asking you to. I'm asking you to let others make assumptions."

It made sense. She could count James as a friend, but until her heart came to its senses, it wouldn't be willing to be offered to anyone except Toby. As that wasn't going to happen, she needed time to figure out what she'd do after he left. No doubt, Menno and Benjamin would redouble their efforts to find her a husband. She had to have a plan in place before their *gut* intentions ruined her life.

"Okay," she said.

"*Danki.*" He raised the reins to tell the horse to drive toward her road a few yards away.

She halted him and got out of the buggy. There was no reason for him to come to the house. Walking up the lane herself would add to the supposition she and James were trying to keep their relationship a secret.

God, danki for having James be so honest with me. Please help my brothers understand their love for me doesn't have to be so overpowering.

Sarah turned to watch James drive away, the metal wheels on his open buggy catching the moonlight. A few minutes later, she smiled as she climbed the stairs to head to bed. Benjamin and Menno were grinning as if they'd won a great victory.

It was a temporary diversion. Eventually they'd take notice, especially if James found someone he wanted to court. For now, she'd appreciate the reprieve. It was a precious gift. She hoped God would soon show her what she should do once Toby left.

The thought sent tears flooding into her eyes. She was grateful he was healing well, but she had no idea how she was going to tell him goodbye.

Chapter Thirteen

"Mr. Summerhays, may I come in?"

Sarah peeked around the corner of her boss's office. When he smiled and motioned for her to enter, she saw he had a phone pressed to his ear.

She tiptoed into the room. Arranged on the dark green wallpaper above the dark wood panels was a collection of photographs of Mr. Summerhays's prize-winning horses. Two horses had been immortalized in oil paintings.

As soon as Mr. Summerhays was done with his call, he pointed to a chair in front of his large desk. "What can I do for you, Sarah? The children are doing well and behaving for you, aren't they?"

Sitting, she wondered what he would say if she spoke from the heart, pleading with him to discover the answer for himself. She'd grasp on to any excuse for him to spend time with his *kinder*, but he would beg off, saying he had important work to do as he had the few times she'd tried to broach the subject.

Toby was correct. If she didn't say something blunt, neither parent was going to see the mistakes they were making by being focused on things other than their youngsters.

Now wasn't the time to mention that. Not if she wanted Mr. Summerhays to agree to a favor.

"I'm here to talk about Toby," she said.

"Who?"

"Toby Christner. The man who injured his ankle and is staying here until J.J. Rafferty comes for him."

Mr. Summerhays's face remained blank.

"Toby is," she said, trying another tack, "the horse trainer who was hurt when unloading Bay Boy."

"Ah! I know whom you're talking about now. What about him? Is he having trouble getting better?"

She silenced her sigh. Mr. Summerhays was focused on his horses and his work in New York City. Nothing else, not even his family.

"No, sir," she said. "He's doing well. In fact, his physical therapist says he's improving faster than expected. That's why I'm here. He's anxious to get back to work."

"That's excellent news. I knew I could depend on you, Sarah, to make sure he was taken care of."

Amazed he recalled he'd asked her to assist Toby, she said, "I'm glad to help. I must admit I told him that he'd get a prize if he met his physical therapy goal." Realizing how that sounded, she hurried to add, "Would you be willing to let him spend a day at the stables near Saratoga if his *doktor* gives him permission to do so? He's interested in seeing your stables there."

Mr. Summerhays frowned. "It's the middle of racing season. I don't have time to babysit someone."

"You wouldn't be babysitting him, sir. You only need to have someone take him there and bring him home at day's end. Toby gets around fine now."

He drummed his fingers on his desk, then looked at his cell phone as it buzzed. His brows lowered. "I'll make sure he gets a tour."

"One other thing? May I cancel the lessons for the *kinder*—the children—tomorrow and take them on a special trip in the buggy?"

"Yes, yes." He waved her out of his office.

Before she had stood, he was talking into his phone. She hurried out, happy Mr. Summerhays had agreed to her requests, but sad he considered taking the call more important than finding out where she planned to take his *kinder*.

Soon, she promised herself. Soon, she'd do as she and Toby had discussed. She would speak to Mr. Summerhays about spending time with the youngsters. She wished she knew how to initiate that topic.

A hint of fall banished the humidity the next morning. Sarah guessed it would return, but, for now, she was going to enjoy the pleasant day. The Summerhays *kinder* should enjoy the treat she had for them. As for Toby…

She wasn't sure what he'd make of the surprise she had planned for the youngsters today. He'd seemed astonished when she asked him to join them for a drive along the road into Harmony Creek Hollow. To be honest, she'd been amazed when he agreed to come.

Charmer stepped along the road, as delighted as Sarah was at the cooler weather. The *kinder* were enjoying the ride and discussing where they might be going.

She didn't realize she was humming until Toby asked, "What tune is that?"

"My happy song," she replied with a smile.

"I'm guessing your date on Sunday night went well."

"It wasn't a date." She wagged a playful finger at him. "You've spent too much time with *Englischers*."

"Enough to know a plain man taking a young woman

home from a youth event, Sarah, is like an *Englischer* asking her to a movie. Lots of darkness and whispering."

She arched a brow at him. "*Ach*, I didn't realize you were an expert."

"I'm not, but you're avoiding answering my question. Just tell me it isn't my business."

"It *isn't* your business, but I'll tell you my date went as I'd hoped it would. James was nice."

"But?"

"You're nosy, you know!"

"As nosy as your brothers?"

Sarah laughed without a hint of humor. "Nowhere near. I told them enough to be honest and keep them from planning another date for us right away." Folding her arms in front of her, she asked, "How was your evening?"

"Not as noteworthy as yours, I'm sure."

Gnawing on her lower lip, she turned away before he could see how his teasing hurt. It'd been barely a day, but she was tired of walking the fine line between truth and lies.

Toby became serious. "Sarah, I'm sorry. I was kidding."

"I know, but I don't like having to watch everything I say or do when I'm home. Not to be honest with my brothers bothers me. They think they're succeeding as matchmakers when I know they're not."

"I thought you said…" Abrupt understanding filled his eyes.

Dismay threatened to strangle her. She and James had agreed to keep their true feelings a secret from everyone else so her brothers didn't push them together all the time. And she had just blurted out the truth to Toby!

"I need you to forget what I just said, Toby."

"About you and James? It's forgotten. As far as your

brothers, you haven't lied to them. You're letting them jump to their own conclusions."

"I know, but under other circumstances I would have corrected them because that's what a loving sister should do."

"Sarah, you *are* a loving sister. If you hadn't been, you wouldn't have agreed when they asked you to let James bring you home. If your brothers fail to see that, then they aren't looking at the situation with clear heads and fair eyes. I'm sorry if I upset you."

He grabbed the reins in front of her hands and pulled the buggy onto the grassy shoulder to the right as a car sped past them. "They drive way too fast along this road."

Sarah calmed the *kinder*, using the time to compose herself, too. She hadn't expected Toby to take the reins as her brothers used to do when she was younger. Being annoyed with him was silly.

Making sure her voice was even, she said, "We've alerted the sheriff, but the patrols can't be here all the time."

Mia leaned over the seat. "Will we be there soon, Sarah?"

"Where?" she asked as she winked at Toby, who struggled to keep a straight face.

"Where we're going!"

"We're there."

The buggy rolled to a stop near the new school building the settlement had opened about six weeks before.

Turning in her seat, Sarah said, "I know you're on summer vacation for another couple of weeks, but would you like to see where your Amish neighbors go to school?"

"Here?" Ethan was eager to start kindergarten and anything about school thrilled him.

"*Ja.*"

"Me, too?" Mia asked. With another year to wait until she went to school, she expected to be left out.

"You, too." Sarah tapped her nose and was rewarded with a grin. "Now, remember you are guests here. You need to use your best manners."

Alexander grimaced. "Aren't they schoolkids like us?"

"They are, but Miriam expects everyone to behave in her school. You know Miriam, and you know she's a nice person. Why don't you ask me your questions about an Amish school so you don't disrupt the class? Anyone got questions?" She smiled at Toby. He knew, as she did, the Summerhays kids *always* had a lot of questions.

"Why have they started school already?" Alexander asked. "We don't go back for two weeks."

"Amish schools need to begin the school year early so they can start their summer vacations in mid-May. That way, the scholars can help their families put in their crops. Maybe the school will go a bit longer here, because the fields won't be ready quite as early, but they'll be done with school by the end of May."

"What's a scholar?" asked Mia.

"A scholar is someone in school."

"Oh, like the ten o'clock scholar in Mia's *Mother Goose* book," Natalie said.

"Exactly."

"How many grades are there?"

"Eight. First grade through eighth grade, as you have at your school."

"We've got kindergarten, too," Ethan said.

Sarah almost laughed when Toby glanced back to give the little boy a wink, which made Ethan stick out his narrow chest with pride. "That's true. Once our scholars have finished eighth grade, they're done with formal education. After that, they may spend time with someone who will teach them a skill like woodworking or running a shop."

"So no high school?" asked Natalie.

"No. We feel it's important to learn a usable skill during those years."

That gave the *kinder* something to think about as they got out of the buggy. Sarah checked they were neat before she led them toward the school.

The new building looked like other plain schools, both outside and in. When Sarah opened the door, walking in as Miriam had asked, she saw the desks the dozen *kinder* used were in rows on the gray linoleum floor. The youngest scholars sat at the front and those in their last year of school had the privilege of having their desks closest to the door, so they could be the first outside for recess and at the end of the day. She recalled how grown-up she'd felt when, at fourteen, she reached the eighth grade and was ready to put school behind her. It'd been an honor, vied for by the oldest students, to clean the erasers and wash the blackboard. These scholars looked so young now.

Miriam stood at her desk on the raised platform in front of a wall covered with blackboard paint. A whiteboard was set on an easel beside her desk, and simple math problems were displayed on it.

"Scholars, our guests have arrived," she said as she walked past the desks toward the door. "Let me greet them, and then we'll introduce everyone."

The tall teacher welcomed Sarah and Toby and the *kinder* to the school. The Summerhays kids grinned when Miriam said how much the scholars were looking forward to playing softball with them during recess.

"First, we have work to do." Miriam called out three names, and two boys and a girl stood.

They were each close to the age of the Summerhays *kinder*. The newcomers looked at Sarah, who nodded, amazed at how shy her usually raucous charges were.

"What about me?" asked Mia. "I'm not old enough for school."

"Mia, *komm* with me." Miriam held out her hand. "I've got a special seat for you."

Soon the *Englisch kinder* were sitting with their plain counterparts and working together on the lessons assigned for the day. Mia sat in the front row with the smallest scholars. She grinned as she bent her head over a workbook and pointed to a picture of a rabbit before she began to color it. As eager as she was to attend school with her older sister and brothers, coming to the one-room schoolhouse was an extra special treat for her.

Sarah smiled as Miriam paused beside her. Keeping her voice low so they didn't disturb the scholars, Sarah said, "*Danki* for letting them come here, Miriam. They're having a *wunderbaar* time. Learning about the lives of their plain neighbors is going to make them comfortable with them."

"Some of the scholars' parents have expressed concern about the Summerhays family offering an invitation in return."

"I understand."

"*Gut.*" Miriam seemed about to add more but went to a student who had a question for her.

In her wake, Sarah's smile vanished. She should have guessed a few of the plain parents wouldn't want their *kinder* spending time at an *Englisch* house where they'd see toys and gadgets that could lure a young person away from an Amish life. Did people think that of her, too? That she was considering leaving because of fancy electronic devices?

She sighed. If she did jump the fence, it would be because of what the *Englisch* world would allow her to do for others, not what enticements it offered to her. Nobody would understand that, either. She prayed her brothers would change their minds, but that was as likely as snow falling on a hot August morning.

Toby stood to one side as the kids ran and squealed during a short afternoon break, tossing leaves into the air and at each other. Most were chattering about the upcoming fair. He knew none of them had gone before, because there hadn't been a settlement last year.

"You look as if you'd like to play with them," said Sarah as she joined him to watch the scholars.

"Why not? They're having a great time, and I always enjoyed recess."

"Did you go to school in Texas? Are their schools similar to ours?"

He shrugged. "I don't know. I was too old for school by the time we moved there. I'm not sure how many schools I went to, though I know one year it was six different ones."

"In one year?"

He nodded.

"I've never heard of anyone who moved six times in one year."

"Now you have."

She blinked when she heard the regret in his voice. He was glad he'd kept the bitterness hidden.

Maybe not well enough, because she said, "I've been curious why your family moved so often."

Toby didn't answer right away. He'd been asked about that as many times as they'd relocated from one district to another. Learning ways to avoid answering had become a habit, but he wanted to be honest with Sarah.

Drawing her closer to the tree so they were less likely to be overheard, he said, "The answer is simple. My *daed* is a man who's sure he knows everything. Well, if not everything, then more than anyone he's talking to."

"Uh-oh." Her eyes widened, and compassion filled them.

"*Ja*, uh-oh describes it. Not many people like being told they are wrong by someone who never doubts his opinions. *Daed* didn't care if the person he was speaking to was *Englisch* or plain or ordained or not. He felt others needed to accept his point of view without question."

"That wouldn't have worked here where everyone is working together to build our *Ordnung*. No one's voice should be louder than anyone else's."

"I agree, but *Daed* wouldn't. If the person he'd cornered didn't agree with him, he tried to browbeat the person into accepting he was right. People got tired of trying to avoid him or being stuck listening to him, so *Daed* would decide it was a waste of time to try to enlighten the others. That's what he always called it. Enlightening the foolish."

"He never saw his mistakes?"

"Never. We would move to a new district, and I'd have such high hopes. This time wouldn't be the same." He sighed. "I know *Mamm* felt that way, too, though she didn't complain—not once—when *Daed* would come home and announce we were leaving for another place where he hoped to find like-minded folks."

"You mean, people who agreed with him."

"That's what he's been looking for." He sighed. "I've tried to forgive him for dragging us from place to place."

"It must have been hard for a *kind* to understand."

"It was. That's why when I found work at J.J.'s ranch I refused to leave with them. I've lost count of how many times they've moved since then."

"You've found the home you've wanted." Her eyes didn't meet his, so he couldn't guess what she was thinking. "No wonder you're so eager for your boss to get you home." She flashed him a feeble smile before going to where her friend was calling the scholars in at recess's end.

Toby didn't move to follow. His gut warned him he'd made a big mistake, but he couldn't guess what it was. Sarah wouldn't judge him for failing to forgive his *daed*, would she? He thought of how many times she'd forgiven her brothers and sighed. He might be able to leave Harmony Creek Hollow without breaking any ties, because it felt as if, with a handful of kind words, she'd severed everything between them.

Chapter Fourteen

The *kinder* sat in the middle seat of Hank Puente's van, except for Ethan, who'd claimed the front seat. The little boy was chattering about the things he planned to do at the county fairgrounds, though he had no idea what would be there. Ethan had asked Sarah a slew of questions during breakfast, and to many she'd had to reply she didn't know. She'd never been to the fairgrounds, either.

Hank, the *Englisch* driver, listened as if everything the *kind* said was of the utmost importance. Sarah guessed he'd heard it many times before from youngsters who were excited about attending the fair.

Mia was half-asleep with her head on Sarah's lap. The little girl had been so wound up last night she hadn't slept well. Smoothing the *kind's* hair toward her braids, Sarah noticed Alexander's head was bobbing, too. She hoped fatigue wouldn't end up making them leave the grounds earlier than she'd planned.

She wished to celebrate the excellent news Toby had received yesterday. His *doktor* was pleased with how Toby's ankle was healing. Though the *doktor* wanted him to continue with physical therapy for another two weeks, Toby now could walk with a cane rather than crutches as long as his ankle wasn't too painful.

She hoped he wouldn't put too much stress on the muscles by leaving his crutches in Salem, so he had to rely only on the cane. Natalie had assured her after checking the particulars on the county fair's website that it would be possible to rent a wheelchair at a booth near the parking lot. The obstacle would be to persuade Toby to use it.

He would acquiesce, she knew. He'd do anything to leave for Texas when J.J. got back to Summerhays Stables. Toby's explanation of his childhood instability and how he'd found what he wanted at the ranch in Texas had made many things clear.

One thing most of all: Toby wouldn't stay any longer than necessary.

Nothing she did could change that, not even if she offered him her heart.

Ethan's cheer from the front seat startled Sarah out of her unwelcome reverie. It also woke his younger sister and announced they'd reached the fairgrounds. The flat open fields were about half a mile from the forested edge of a cliff that dropped to the Hudson River and the village of Schuylerville. Buildings, many of them long, low barns with open sides, were painted white and set in neat rows on either side of a pedestrian road. Smaller booths and rides covered with bulbs trying to outglow the sunshine were close to the road leading to the parking area.

The fairgrounds teemed with people there to enjoy the games, rides and exhibits. Through the van's open windows came the scents of onions and peppers cooking on grills.

She stretched forward to hand Hank the passes Mr. Summerhays had given her before they left. Her boss hadn't said where he obtained them, but she guessed they'd come from someone in the horse-training community.

"There's one for you, too, Hank," she said, "if you want to stay."

"Thanks, but I've got a bunch of other folks waiting to be brought here." He held one ticket over his shoulder.

She shook her head. "Keep it and let someone use it."

"Thanks." He leaned his elbow on the window and greeted the teenage boy selling tickets. "Two adults and four kids. I'm dropping them off."

"Sure thing, Hank." The boy waved as the van drove past him.

Even with their seat belts on, the Summerhays *kinder* twisted in their seats, trying to see everything from the midway to the animal barns as Hank drove toward the parking lot beyond the last row of buildings. The van bounced hard into chuckholes that were invisible in the long, matted grass.

They stopped by one end of the parked cars. Hank got out and slid the side door open while Sarah helped Mia with her seat belt. By the time the little girl was ready to step out, her siblings were waiting for her. Sarah jumped out and swung Mia to the ground.

No one spoke as Toby lowered himself from the van with the help of his cane. He winced when he put weight on his right ankle but steadied himself as he shifted his balance to his left side.

Alexander jumped forward to shut the door once Toby moved away. He slapped the side of the van and waved to Hank, who'd climbed back in.

Making sure the *kinder* were watching out for the many vehicles, Sarah herded them toward the first row of buildings. The pens inside held a variety of farm animals. Pigs were displayed right in front of them in the nearest building, while pens at the other end of the building held goats. Sounds of cows, chickens and sheep came from other open-sided buildings. Among them, the youngsters who'd entered the animals for judging were feeding and tending them.

"Those are the cleanest pigs I've ever seen," Sarah said as the *kinder* paused to admire a huge pig in the outermost pen.

"The judges want to see every inch of them," a boy replied as he scrubbed his entry with soapy water and a brush. "They've got to look their best." He chuckled. "And smell their best."

Once they were past the road filled with a steady stream of cars and trucks headed for the parking lot, Sarah let the *kinder* walk in front of them. She asked Toby how he was doing with the cane.

"The uneven ground is more of a challenge than I'd anticipated," he replied.

"If you want to sit—"

"No, the *doktor* said it was important to exercise my ankle now that it's healed enough to put stress on it."

"Not too much stress. The muscles need time to heal."

"Okay, *Doktorfraa* Kuhns."

She smiled, because that was what he'd expect her to do. Wallowing in her grief that within a couple of weeks he'd be leaving would ruin the day the *kinder* had looked forward to.

What gut will it do, Lord? I'm at fault for not listening to Toby from the beginning when he was honest with me. I know You have a plan for each of us, and, though I wish it, Your plan doesn't seem to have Toby and me being together. Please help me accept that.

It was for the best, she told herself. Until she knew

whether she was going to remain in the settlement, she couldn't make any other plans.

"What do you want to do first?" she asked in order to escape her thoughts.

All four answered at once.

Raising her hands, she waited for them to stop. "Okay, let's try that again. Natalie, what do you want to do first?"

"It's almost nine. Let's go watch them judge the sheep."

Alexander crowed, "You want to see Nick!"

As his sister turned the color of the strawberries on her shirt, Sarah said, "Now, enough teasing. You all like Nick and will hope he does well."

"Nick?" asked Toby.

"He attends their private school that's halfway between Salem and Cambridge. He's in Natalie's class. They live about five miles north of the stables, and their *mamm* has been taking the Summerhays *kinder* to school for as long as I've worked there." She lowered her voice. "I've tried to arrange time for him and Alexander to play this summer, but either one or the other of them is busy every minute of every day."

"That's a shame. The *kinder* enjoy picking on each other, ain't so?"

"It's because they love each other so much. They wouldn't tease each other as they do otherwise."

"Or you."

Warmth swept through her as they neared the judging area. "When I first began taking care of them, I didn't see their pranks as anything except troublemaking. They were angry at being handed off again. Now, when they tease me, they have twinkles in their eyes."

"There's Nick," shouted Ethan, his voice carrying over everyone else's.

The boy leading a sheep with circular horns into the open area glanced toward them and grinned. Natalie hunched into herself, so Sarah put a bolstering arm around her shoulders.

"Don't distract him, Ethan," Toby said. "Nick needs to concentrate on showing off his entry to the judges."

The little boy nodded but clung to the fence. He was fascinated by the parade of sheep with girls and boys. Most of the kids were preteen or younger.

"I love sheep," Ethan announced to nobody in particular.

"Do you think your boss will agree when his younger son asks to raise sheep?" asked Toby.

"By the time we leave the fair, Ethan will have changed his mind a dozen times and set his heart on several other animals for pets."

"Kids that age are fickle."

"They are."

"It's a *gut* thing we outgrow that, ain't so?" he asked in a husky whisper that teased her cheek beyond her bonnet.

Warmth squeezed her heart, though his words could be a warning of his intentions not to be diverted from the life he'd built for himself in Texas. The rough edge of his voice offered an invitation she longed to accept. It would lead to worse heartache, but why not let her heart delight in this moment?

She remained next to Toby throughout the judging. They cheered when Nick was awarded second place and received a bright red ribbon. The blue ribbon went to the girl standing beside him. When they shook hands, the crowd cheered louder.

"I think there's fried dough waiting for us to sample it," Toby said, grinning.

"Don't get too far ahead," Sarah called as the kids took off as if rocket-propelled.

"We'll catch them at the fried-dough stand."

"If something else doesn't grab their attention on the way."

Toby wasn't surprised Sarah's joke of warning was proved true. By the time the *kinder* finished sampling fried dough, burgers and three flavors of ice cream, they were eager to visit the midway and the rides.

While Sarah went to the booth to buy tickets for them, he listened to the youngsters debate which ride they'd go on first.

Mia, Ethan and Natalie agreed it should be the merry-go-round. Toby guessed the thrilling rides seemed too scary for the younger *kinder*, and Natalie was fascinated by anything with horses, real or wooden.

"The carousel?" scoffed Alexander. "It's for little kids. I want to go on the snap-the-whip. Why can't we go on that first?"

"Want to ride the horsies first." Mia propped her fists on her hips and glowered at her older brother.

"We'll be trying a bunch of the rides," said Sarah when she rejoined them. "Let's start with the carousel, and then we'll decide which ride will be next."

Alexander glowered for a second but was grinning again by the time they reached the merry-go-round. As Sarah handed tickets to the man running it, she looked at Toby, "Do you think you can handle these horses, cowboy?"

"I'm not—" He laughed. "I guess I prefer to be called a cowboy instead of 'horse-boy' as Alexander suggested."

"Trust you to say something like that, Alexander."

She ruffled the boy's hair, and he chuckled, his annoyance forgotten.

Toby lifted Mia onto a bright pink horse. When she giggled and grabbed the reins as if she could make the horse go right then, he turned to watch Ethan scramble onto a gold horse next to Mia's. Natalie chose a white horse, while Alexander climbed on an alligator. It was the only non-horse on the merry-go-round, but Toby wasn't surprised the boy had found it. Alexander was resolved to go his own way in life, no matter how strange it might be.

"Shall we ride in the shell?" asked Sarah. "It's the ladylike thing to do."

He appreciated how she pretended, so he wouldn't have to worry about his ankle while getting on and off a painted horse.

She selected the double seat behind where the *kinder* were perched, so she could keep an eye on them. It was painted bright pink and yellow.

He bent his head so he didn't bang it on the edge of the shell, which resembled the froth off a wave. Dropping beside her, he grimaced.

"You *are* doing better, you know," she said.

"I'd like to be doing *gut*."

"You will be. Last week, you were on crutches. Now you've got a cane."

He did not want to admit he wished he had his crutches because his right ankle ached on every step. If he complained, he guessed Sarah would cut their day short. He didn't want that.

The ride began moving, and Sarah bumped against him. She edged away, and he wished she hadn't. How easily he could have curled his fingers around her shoulder! To do so would be announcing a commitment he couldn't offer her, not if he intended to hold on to the life he'd built on J.J.'s ranch.

Was that the life he wanted?

He couldn't recall the last time he'd felt so content. *Content* was a word he used to despise, but no longer. He wasn't obligating himself to anything but enjoying the moment with Sarah and four outrageous *Englisch kinder.*

Danki, God, for this day and these people.

The prayer startled Toby. Not that he'd prayed, but that speaking to God seemed wondrously familiar. He'd missed it more than he'd realized.

Listening to Sarah hum the simple melody coming from the center of the carousel, he found himself doing the same. He wasn't sure what the name of the tune was, but he thought it might go along with a nursery rhyme. Ahead of them, the *kinder* were laughing as the horses and alligator rose and fell.

"Summerhays is foolish to miss this," he said.

"I agree."

"Why can't he see how much his kids want to spend time with him and his wife?" He answered his question before she could. "Maybe they'd know if they spent more time with their *kinder.*"

"Mia used to disappear, and I'd have to find her because she needed to eat. I would search but had to give up because her sister and brothers needed me. Then I discovered she hides in her *mamm's* closet." Sarah sighed. "The other three vie for their *daed's* time, but days go by without them seeing him."

"We've got to be halfway to his stables in Saratoga."

"We are."

"It didn't take half an hour for us to get here, so why can't he get home to spend time with his family?"

"I don't know. I've worked for the man for nine

months, and I don't know much about him or his wife.
Other than when they hired me, I haven't spoken with
either of them for more than an hour or two total."

Toby hid his astonishment and said nothing until the
ride slowed to a stop. He got out of the seat while Sarah
helped the littler ones from their horses.

Mia grabbed his hand as they walked down the steps
at the exit. Looking at him, she said, "That was fun,
ain't so?"

"Ja," he said, glad he could speak from the heart. "And
the right speed for a man with a cane."

That made the *kinder* giggle, but his heart focused on
the music of Sarah's laugh. It soared through him, as free
and beautiful as an eagle's flight.

As the *kinder* surrounded her, each one asking to go
on a different ride, he stepped aside and smiled. Now he
couldn't be alone with Sarah, but he was going to find a
way to do so. They didn't have much time before he had
to leave. He wanted to take advantage of every second.

Toby tried not to think of how many eyes were watching his slow progress among the picnic tables. Sarah followed him, and he guessed her hands were outstretched
to catch him if he started to wobble. In front of him, Alexander was walking backward, prepared to keep Toby
from falling onto his nose.

"Slow and steady wins the race," Alexander said in
tempo with the bump of the cane and Toby's footsteps.

"Do you believe that?" Toby grinned at the boy. "I
can't believe your *daed* does."

"You aren't a racehorse." Alexander chuckled. "By
the way, it's Sarah who says that, not my father." A cloud
passed across the boy's face for a moment as he men-

tioned his *daed*. In its wake, Alexander avoided looking at him.

As soon as Toby was sitting at a wooden table, Ethan held out a plastic cup of lemonade to him. Taking the sticky cup, which warned that Ethan's attempts not to splash the lemonade hadn't been successful, Toby thanked him. He guided the *kind* to where he could sit so more didn't spill.

Taking a sip of the lemonade, Toby listened to Sarah chat with the youngsters. He thought of how she'd said Summerhays had spent less time talking to her about his *kinder* than he had to Toby about Bay Boy and the other horses at the stables in Salem. How could that be? Summerhays must be able to see how much his *kinder* wanted to spend time with him. Toby had noticed that shortly after he'd arrived at the stables.

People could train themselves to ignore what they didn't want to see. His *daed* had been an expert at that, refusing to believe he was making the same mistakes.

Toby wasn't done with his lemonade when Sarah handed a strip of tickets to Natalie. The *kinder* rushed off to get in line to ride the nearby miniature train.

"I thought you'd like to sit a little bit longer," she said to him as she folded her arms on the table.

"*Danki.* A few minutes more, and I should be able to walk the length of the midway so they can ride on the snap-the-whip."

"We'll see about that." She straightened. "Listen to me. I sound like my brothers, always worrying too much. The kids are big enough for that ride."

"Your brothers do worry a lot about you."

"All the time." She shook her head and turned toward where fire trucks and other emergency vehicles were parked so the fair-goers could examine them. "Too much.

They don't believe a plain woman should be involved as a first responder."

"And you want to?"

"Ja."

"You want to be a firefighter?"

She shook her head. "I want to train as an EMT. I know it's ridiculous, but it's something I feel God is drawing me toward."

"It's not ridiculous." He shouldn't have been surprised. She'd been interested in his physical therapy and had asked questions every session. She clearly had plenty of medical knowledge already.

"Benjamin and Menno think so. They've forbidden me from taking the training." Resentment slipped into her voice. "They said it isn't an appropriate thing for a plain woman to do."

"I've lived in plenty of plain communities, and many of them had plain women working with the volunteer ambulance services. In two, plain women served as firefighters."

Hope brightened her face. "I should tell them." The hope seeped away as she added, "Why? They won't listen to me. They don't believe Amish women do such things."

Shock pierced him. "So are you considering leaving the Amish?"

She nodded.

"Is that why you're working as a nanny? To learn more about *Englischers*?"

"It started out as an opportunity to do that, but now I do it because I love the *kinder*."

"If your brothers agreed to let you take the EMT training, would you stay on the Amish side of the fence?"

"They won't let me. End of story."

"Do you want my opinion?"

"Ja." The corners of her lips tilted. "Though I suspect you're going to give it to me, whether I want it or not."

"If you didn't want to hear it, I'd keep it to myself. As you do, here it goes. My opinion is Sarah Kuhns can do anything she puts her mind to. You need to figure out with God's help what that is."

Sarah blinked the sudden tears in her eyes. Toby couldn't guess how *wunderbaar* his words were as they fell like a healing rain on her heart. Someone believed she was capable of following her dreams. Even if she decided to remain among the Amish, this moment would stay with her the rest of her life.

She replayed his words in her mind through the rest of the day. They visited the exhibits and ate junk food before playing games and standing in ever-longer lines for more rides. Though the *kinder* were exhausted by the time Hank returned after dark to take them home, she was sure they had enjoyed every part of the fair.

Letting the youngsters stretch out on the seats, Sarah sat in the rear with Toby. His broad fingers swallowed her smaller hand, and tingles rolled in waves up her arm. She gazed at him, though he was no more than a silhouette in the darkness.

When he drew her toward him, she stared at his lips that were visible in the light of a passing car. They tilted in a smile, and she couldn't halt her eyes from following the firm line of his nose. In his warm eyes, sparks of heat teased her closer. He caressed her cheek, eliciting a melody from deep in her heart. As his mouth lowered, she closed her eyes in sweet anticipation. His strong arms enveloped her at the moment his lips found hers. Everything she'd imagined—and so much more—was in that kiss.

She savored it more because it might be the only one they'd ever share.

He lifted his mouth away, and she leaned her cheek on his shoulder. For one special moment, she was going to forget the past and not think about the future and savor being close to the man she knew she'd love the rest of her life, whether they were together or not.

Chapter Fifteen

"Sarah?"

"Sarah?"

Hearing her name called a second time—or was it more times than that?—Sarah pulled herself out of the delicious memory of the moment from four days ago when Toby had drawn her into his arms and kissed her while coming home from the fair. She wondered if he would have taken advantage of the shadows among the berry bushes today and kissed her again.

Toby wasn't with them. He'd left at dawn to visit the stables near Saratoga today. His *doktor* had given him permission to spend the day there as long as he did his exercises and put his leg up if his ankle swelled. She hoped Toby was having an amazing time, talking with other trainers and seeing the horses.

"Sarah, are you listening?" asked Alexander as he came around a black raspberry bush.

"She's off in dreamland," Ethan answered.

The *kinder* laughed.

Natalie said through her giggles, "Sarah, your brain has fled your head."

"Sorry." She gave them a smile. "I was lost in thought. Have you picked a lot of berries?"

The *kinder* dumped the contents of their small pails of black raspberries into her larger bucket. The plop of every juicy berry made her mouth water.

"How many more do we need to get?" asked Natalie.

Hefting the bucket, she said, "I'd say we're there. Mrs. Beebe said we needed about six cups of berries for the cobbler she's going to make for your dessert."

The youngsters' cheers sent a flock of small birds fleeing into the sky.

Sarah took their pails along with hers and grabbed Mia's hand as they walked through the field beyond the pastures. She smiled when Natalie took Ethan's hand without being instructed. Perhaps the older *kinder* were beginning to understand the joy of helping each other.

"How will Mrs. Beebe cook our berries?" asked Ethan, always eager for the details.

"She'll wash them and mix them with sugar. Next, she'll make the cobbler with flour and more sugar and butter. After putting the cobbler on top of the berries, she'll bake it in the oven. You'll want to eat every bite of your supper so you can have dessert tonight."

"What are we having?"

She struggled to keep her lips from twitching. "Liver."

Fervent shouts of "No!" and "You're kidding!" made her laugh. The *kinder* knew then she was teasing them. The joking continued as they walked across the road to the drive leading to their home.

Mrs. Beebe greeted them warmly in the partially finished kitchen. A huge new gas stove sat in the middle of the floor, waiting to be swapped with the slightly smaller one that couldn't be more than a year or two old. Somehow, the cook continued to make meals for the family and the staff while new cabinets were hung and counters set into place.

"She's back," Mrs. Beebe murmured to Sarah while taking the buckets.

"She?"

"Her ladyship."

Baffled, Sarah started to ask another question.

As if on cue, a delicate voice called from the front hall. "I'm home! Where is everyone?"

Sarah gasped, realizing the cook had been referring to Mrs. Summerhays. The sound was lost beneath excited shrieks from the *kinder*. They raced toward the front of the house.

"Like I said, her ladyship's home," Mrs. Beebe said in response to Sarah's unspoken question. "She got here about a half hour after you and the children left." Stirring a pot on the stove, she smiled. "You'd better get in there and make sure they don't run roughshod over her."

Sarah nodded and hurried out of the kitchen. She'd spoken with Mrs. Summerhays fewer than a half-dozen times in the months she'd been working at the house, because even when the woman was home, she was busy elsewhere.

When she went into the entry, Sarah watched the *kinder* greet their *mamm*. Mrs. Summerhays was willowy. Every motion was so light it seemed to float like a branch on a gentle breeze. She reminded Sarah of a ballerina in one of Mia's storybooks. As if at any moment, she could rise to the tips of her toes and waft about to music.

As always, Mrs. Summerhays was dressed in an elegant style that matched the grandeur of her home. Her ivory coat had the sheen of silk. The fancy purse she carried, though Mrs. Beebe had reported Mrs. Summerhays had been home for an hour, was the exact same black as her stilettos. Each heel was no wider than a pencil, but Mrs. Summerhays didn't wobble. She wore those shoes as she did everything, with a confidence of knowing she looked stylish.

Sarah watched as Mrs. Summerhays hugged her *kinder*. She held each briefly, keeping them from putting their cheeks against her coat. No doubt, she didn't want to chance staining the elegant fabric.

Tears welled in Sarah's eyes. What would Mrs. Summerhays say if Sarah told her how much she was missing out on? Each enthusiastic dirty-faced hug and kiss Sarah received from the *kinder* was precious, because she knew how difficult it'd been for them—at first—to open up to her.

"Look at how you've grown," their *mamm* exclaimed. "Mrs. Beebe must be feeding you bean sprouts, because you're sprouting."

The *kinder* grinned. Those expressions faltered when Mrs. Summerhays stepped away, but the youngsters dutifully cheered when she announced she'd brought them gifts from Europe and put them in Mia's room. She encouraged them to check out what she'd bought them. For a moment, the *kinder* hesitated, and Sarah knew they didn't want to leave their *mamm* when they'd just said hello.

"Go! Go!" Mrs. Summerhays made dismissive waves toward the stairs. "I need to go out, but I should be back before you go to bed."

Natalie halted. "Mom, we picked black raspberries and Mrs. Beebe's gonna make cobbler."

"You've been busy." She laughed. "Enjoy the fruits of your labors."

The *kinder* glanced at one another, puzzled, but scurried away when their *mamm* urged them to look at their gifts upstairs. Mrs. Summerhays's enthusiasm must have rubbed off on them, because the youngsters chattered with excitement, their high-pitched voices reverberating off every corner of the high ceilings.

Mrs. Summerhays smiled at Sarah. "From what Ian tells me, you've been keeping them under control, Sarah. You're just what they need."

What they need is their mamm *and* daed.

Sarah halted the words before they escaped. Instead, she smiled and replied, "They've been looking forward to you arriving home before school starts."

"I can't believe Mia is heading off to school full-time, too."

"Mia won't be attending school until next year."

"Oh." Mrs. Summerhays looked nonplussed; then she composed her face into a smile again. "I meant Ethan. He's going to school this year, isn't he?"

"Yes, he is, and he's excited. He'll be glad you're here for his first day of school."

"I *hope* I will." She took a step toward the front door. "I'll know more after this evening's meeting with other owners' spouses. Do check on the children. By the way, I left a gift for you in Mia's room."

Then she was gone, the door closing behind her.

Sarah stared, speechless. She'd delayed too long in finding a way to speak to Mr. and Mrs. Summerhays about spending more time with their *kinder*. It was time to rectify that.

Tomorrow.

For now, she must go and see how the *kinder* fared.

As she climbed the stairs, she noticed how a peculiar hush had settled on the house. The youngsters' exuberant voices were silent. She passed Mrs. Hancock in the upper hallway and sighed when the housekeeper shook her head sadly and hurried to the first floor.

Sarah paused. Would Mrs. Hancock help her find the

best way to approach their boss to discuss what the *kinder* longed for?

That discussion was for later. Now...

She paused by the doorway of Mia's room. It was a big space with its white-and-pink-striped wallpaper. The room shared a bath with Natalie's bedroom that was decorated in everything horse.

Near the wide window, the *kinder* sat among scraps of the paper that had wrapped their gifts. The gifts themselves were stacked on Mia's bed. Sarah saw clothing and toys as well as a half-dozen books. Even the books about horses were piled with the others. As she watched, Natalie stood and sighed as she put a ceramic horse that could have been modeled after Bay Boy on the bed before wandering to the window seat and climbing on it so she could see out as she hugged Ethan, whose lower lip was quivering.

Sarah kept her sigh silent. *Lord, You brought me to this family. Please show me how I can help them become a true family like my brothers and I used to be.*

A new wave of sorrow rushed over her. Not so many years ago, Benjamin and Menno had made her feel important to them as Natalie did with the younger two. They hadn't acted as if she were an unwanted burden they couldn't wait to be done with. She missed that time.

"What a generous *mamm* you have!" she said as she entered the room.

If the *kinder* suspected she was pretending to be excited about the gifts, they gave her no sign. She could tell, however, the *kinder* were faking their excitement, too. The clothing was lovely and the perfect size. The toys and books had been chosen well.

She knew they would have traded every gift for a chance to spend just a minute more with their *mamm*.

* * *

It had been an unbelievable day. The aromas of hay, leather, horses and hard work filled every breath Toby drew from when he'd arrived just after dawn. Those odors made him homesick for the stables on J.J.'s ranch. He'd spent hours in and around them every day, except Sundays. Although on Sunday evenings, he was often found working with the horses.

Instead of savoring the chance to be among people who shared his obsession with training horses and the creatures themselves, he kept losing himself in thoughts of Sarah and their kiss. He grinned each time he thought about it. If the other trainers and grooms thought he was a grinning fool, he didn't care.

He'd looked for an opportunity to hold her again, but none had arisen. The one time he thought he might steal another kiss, the *kinder* had come looking for her. That he'd seen disappointment in her eyes before she turned to the youngsters had suggested she regretted the lost opportunity as much as he did.

Toby felt his grin grow wider and wider as he clumped along with his cane in Summerhays's wake at the day's end. The stable's owner had offered him a ride back to the house while on his way to Salem. Summerhays was leaving earlier than usual because he had a meeting to attend.

Horses poked their heads out of their stalls to discover who was making the strange sounds. Though Toby doubted he was the first one to walk with a cane in front of the stable doors, he'd gotten the horses' attention.

He paused and admired a sleek gray who moved along the pasture fence with the grace of a cloud in a bright blue sky. "Aren't you a handsome fellow!"

"You've got a good eye, Christner," Summerhays said. "He's my best. He's been entered in two races and came in first in one and second in the other. He'll be three next year, so I'm going to see that he gets high-visibility races."

Toby was pleased the man continued to discuss his favorite topic as they went to a white truck, which was bigger than the red one Toby had driven to Fleetwood's farm with Sarah and Mercy. When Summerhays asked his opinion on the horses he'd seen, Toby replied honestly. He could tell, as they drove north, Summerhays didn't appreciate all his comments.

Too bad. Toby knew the dangers of misrepresenting a horse and what it was able to do. Mishandling a young horse could mean it never would reach its potential. Thoughtless training might ruin a horse. He'd tried to retrain such horses, but too often they were beyond saving.

"That's an interesting take on the horse," Summerhays said when they discussed the horses at the stables near Harmony Creek Hollow. "You seem to know a lot about my horses after such a short time."

"I had an inside expert share information on the animals in your stables."

"Who?"

"Natalie."

Summerhays, shocked, looked at Toby. Cutting his eyes back to the road, he asked, "My daughter?"

"*Ja.* She knows more about horses and their training than a lot of adults I've worked with."

"You don't say," Mr. Summerhays drawled, pride sifting into his voice. "When do you think Bay Boy will be ready to come down to Saratoga for training?"

"I'd say you could start him here next month. He may be the finest horse I've trained," Toby replied, then smiled. "Natalie agrees."

The older man looked startled, then grinned. "You

may be right about her knowing more than many equine experts. So you've done all you can with him?"

"I've worked with Mick and Cecil and showed them how best to work with Bay Boy," he replied, realizing that Summerhays might be proud of Natalie, but all his thoughts were on his horses. "They know how he hates being in the trailer so much that he refuses to run at his top speed for several days afterward." He glanced at the older man. "You're going to have to keep that in mind. It's not a normal situation, but he's not a normal horse. He knows his mind and thinks he's the boss. Once I let him think I believed it, too, he's been much more cooperative."

Mr. Summerhays nodded. "That makes sense."

"Why are you asking me? You've got experienced grooms and trainers at your stables."

"Too often they give me the answers they think I want to hear, not the truth." He chuckled. "You've heard that, haven't you?"

"Sir?"

"I'm sure Sarah clued you in." Not waiting for a response, he said, "She's one of a kind, Toby."

"Yes, sir."

"That sounds like an answer you give when you don't want to be honest."

Astonished, Toby said, "No, I was agreeing. She *is* one of a kind." He'd never meet another woman like her, no matter how far and wide he searched. But his life was in Texas, and hers was… Abrupt shame pierced him. Too late, he realized he shouldn't have kissed her. No matter how incredible it'd been, it had been a mistake, suggesting a promise he couldn't keep.

"Without her help," Summerhays said, interrupting his appalling thoughts, "I doubt you would have gotten on your feet as quickly."

"True," he answered, holding on to the conversation as a way to keep from thinking about the mess he'd made. "She isn't hesitant to say what is the right thing to do and make sure you do it."

"My kids have given her a lot of practice, no doubt."

Toby knew the horseman's words were the perfect opening for him to share Sarah's concerns about how the *kinder* needed more time with their parents. He almost said something but halted. Sarah had asked him to let her handle it, and he needed to do that. He wouldn't be like her brothers. Protective of her to the point that she was suffocating.

He wasn't thinking clearly at the moment as his emotions roiled through him like clouds in a thunderstorm.

Dropped off in front of the house a half hour later, Toby went inside after Summerhays had turned the truck around and headed toward Salem. Sarah stood in the entry. He didn't need to look at her face to know she was upset. The rigid angle of her shoulders and how her fingers were curling and uncurling by her sides warned him she was trying to calm her feelings before they burst out of her. Something or someone had upset her.

Who?

Had her thoughts followed the same path as his? Did she regret their kiss?

As if he'd asked those questions aloud, Sarah said, "I hoped to talk to you before you ran into the *kinder*. Their *mamm* arrived home this afternoon but spent less than five minutes with them before she had to leave for a meeting. They're having supper, and I don't think they've eaten a single bite."

Shocked, because Alexander could always be counted on to eat everything in front of him, Toby tried to imagine what the *kinder* were feeling. He couldn't. His parents had always kept him at the heart of their family. More than once, he'd heard his *daed* say they were moving to a place where life should be better for Toby. The constant search for a place where his *daed* would find kindred spirits had been aimed at the best life for all of them.

"That's sad," he said, unsure what she needed to hear.

"I plan to speak to Mrs. Summerhays tomorrow. I've been praying on this, Toby."

"I have been, too."

"You have? You seemed distant from God."

"He has never been distant from me. When I look in your eyes, I know He loves me. Otherwise, He wouldn't have given us this chance to be together. How can I not be grateful for His knowing my heart when I didn't?"

"I'm so happy for you," she said, hoping he meant his heart was filled with the same love that was within hers.

"I know you are. You've made me happy, Sarah, just as you have the *kinder*."

"*Ja*, they enjoy being with me, but I'm a poor substitute for their parents. The *kinder* want to be with their *daed* and *mamm*." Her gaze turned inward. "It's been three years since my *daed* died and more than a decade since my *mamm* did, and I would trade anything to have a few minutes more with them in this life."

"I know what you mean. When I stayed at J.J.'s, I had no idea how much I'd miss my folks."

"You should tell them that."

"I know, but I can't figure out how."

She grasped his arms. "Toby, you have to forgive your *daed* for the past. If you do that, you will find the words."

"I don't know if I can." How could he explain the years of hurt that had piled layer upon layer inside him?

"Pray. God will guide you. Please don't wait. If I'd waited to tell my parents how much I loved them…" She snapped her arms together across her chest and glowered. "Don't wait, Toby. Don't be like this family. I see them squandering their chance to be together."

Before he could reply, a phone rang in Summerhays's office. Toby waited in the foyer for Sarah to answer it and return. His arms ached to hold her close until she could push aside her sorrow.

"Toby?" Sarah's voice intruded into his thoughts. "The call is for you."

"For me?"

She nodded. "The man asked for Toby Christner."

He gave her what he hoped was a bolstering smile. "I'll be right back."

Sarah sat on the bottom step of the grand staircase and prayed for God to give her the right words at the right time—and soon!—to talk with the *kinder's* parents. *Open their hearts to hearing the truth so they can build a true relationship with the* kinder *who adore them.*

The sound of Toby's cane against the stone floor brought her head up. God had blessed her by bringing this man into her life to remind her that what she said and did mattered. She was grateful for how well he'd healed...and how her heart had danced like stardust in the moonlight when he kissed her.

"That was J.J. He and Ned are on their way here," he said in an emotionless voice.

Her heart plummeted into her stomach. "When will they get here?"

"Early tomorrow."

His answer burned her like acid. "How long are they staying?"

"Long enough to pick me up."

Disbelief froze her heart. Somehow, she stood. "So

you're leaving tomorrow?" Her words sounded as if they were coming through a long tunnel.

"*Ja.*"

She waited for him to add something.

He didn't. Nor would he meet her gaze.

When she couldn't handle the silence, she said, "I understand." She wished it were the truth.

"You don't need to worry." He wore the same expression Ethan did when he hoped she'd overlook a jam he'd gotten into. "I'm done with our portion of training Bay Boy."

Her brows lowered. "What does the horse have to do with anything?"

"The plan was for one of us to stay and show Summerhays's men what training the horse was accustomed to. So I would have been here, even if I hadn't hurt my ankle. I wasn't going to leave Ned with a pretty woman like you."

"You weren't going to…" She couldn't get the words out.

"Trust me. I know Ned, and you don't."

"You could have warned me." She backed away. "But no, you thought I needed you to protect me."

"It's not that."

"No? Then what do you call making decisions for someone who can make her own decisions?"

"Like I said, I know Ned, and I didn't want you to get hurt."

Tears filled her eyes, but she blinked them away. Would he be like her brothers and see her honest emotions as a sign of weakness?

Taking a steadying breath, she asked, "Why weren't you honest later?"

"It wasn't an issue. Ned was gone, and I was stuck here."

Stuck?

Was that how he saw the time they'd spent together? Had she been nothing more to him than a way to keep from being bored while he was recovering? Worse, knowing he was leaving, he'd kissed her as if she were special to him. She'd shared her dreams with him and offered him her heart.

"I should go," she said. *Before I say something I may or may not regret.*

"Sarah—"

She didn't wait to hear more. He'd said enough to let her know she might have managed again to escape a life of being told what to do and having her decisions denounced as silly or useless. She should have been happy.

It took every bit of her strength to keep from crying while she hurried into the kitchen to check on the *kinder*. She would hold her tears in until later when she was out of the house and too far away for anyone to hear her weep.

Chapter Sixteen

Go to sleep.

Sarah ignored the *gut* advice in her head as she turned over her pillow, looking for a cooler surface that would help her fall asleep before sunrise. She needed to be at work before breakfast, because Mrs. Summerhays intended to travel with her husband to New York City first thing in the morning.

It had taken Sarah an hour to calm the *kinder* after she was sent to tell them that their *mamm* was leaving them again less than a day after she'd returned from Europe. If Mrs. Summerhays had seen their faces that displayed shock and hurt, would she have changed her mind?

Sarah was no longer certain.

Of anything.

On one hand, it was horrible to have someone you loved stifling your dreams at every turn. It was worse to have someone you loved leave you behind so that person could pursue his or her dreams.

As Mr. and Mrs. Summerhays were with their *kinder.*

As Toby was with her.

No, she didn't want to think about Toby. He personified both extremes, going to ridiculous lengths to protect her, though she knew he hadn't injured his ankle on purpose, and now planning to leave without a backward glance. He'd learned all about leaving from his parents.

This time, her tears refused to be kept in her eyes. They streamed down her cheeks, dampening the pillow-case. She tried to dash them away, but they kept falling.

Throwing aside the quilt on her bed, she sat and rubbed her wet cheeks. She rose and paced the small bedroom. She loved her room. The white maple furniture had been brought from Indiana, and the connection with what had been was important to her.

Such connections were what Toby fought at every turn. How could he believe the way to keep himself from being hurt was to hold everyone at a distance? He seemed to believe an endless parade of little hurts was better than a single powerful one.

Maybe he was right, because she'd been torturing herself with her uncertainty about what she should do with her life. Was it better to make a hasty decision and rip away any doubt like tearing a bandage off a healing wound?

She raised her eyes toward the ceiling. *Your will be done, Lord. I know You have a plan for Toby and me, and it isn't for us to be together. Help me come to accept Your will, but please heal his heart. He is too gut a man to be in such constant pain.*

She climbed into bed, knowing she'd poured out everything in her heart and the situation was in God's hands. As it always had been. Letting go eased the tension aching across her shoulders, so she was able to lie on her pillow.

Sleep refused to give her an escape from her thoughts that went around and around as the carousel had at the fair. Was there something more she could have done to persuade Toby that fleeing from any relationship wouldn't lead him to where he wanted to be? Maybe he was too used to saying goodbye.

The room was stuffy, but it was too chilly to open the window. At least the summer heat had been banished for the night. Sarah closed her eyes and tried to keep her mind from drifting in a dozen directions.

It seemed minutes later, but it must have been a few hours because the moon had fallen to hide halfway behind the mountains along the western horizon. Its light crossed the foot of Sarah's bed as her eyes popped open at a horrifying sound.

Sirens!

Fire sirens!

She sat straight up in bed, then ran to her window. Throwing it open, she pressed her ear to the screen. The siren rose and fell again and again, each shriek sounding more frantic.

The siren on the top of the library building in Salem!

A flash of light reached under her bedroom door before vanishing toward the stairs. As she grabbed her robe, whipping it around her, she heard Benjamin urge Menno to hurry.

She opened her door so hard it slammed against the wall. Her brothers paused in astonishment as she burst from her room.

"Where is it?" she called.

Benjamin looked at the pager at his waist. It alerted him when there was an emergency. "The code says it's east of the village."

"Where?"

"Along the road to Rupert." He blanched as the beeper sounded again. "2127 Old Route 153. Isn't that—"

"Summerhays Stables!"

They shared a gasp of shock.

Menno grasped her shoulders. "Stay here, Sarah," he ordered. "You aren't trained, and you would just be in the way."

Her brothers ran down the stairs and out the door, slamming it behind them, before she could retort that she could have been a great help if he and Benjamin had let her become an EMT.

No matter! She wasn't going to wait. She'd stay out of the way, but she knew which bedrooms the *kinder* used and the best way to get to them. Surely the firefighters would appreciate such information.

Running into her room, she pulled on clothes and grabbed a flashlight out of the table by her bed. She ran down the stairs as soon as her shoes were tied. The door crashed closed behind her. As she ran toward the woods, she heard their buggy careening at top speed along the road. Other people and vehicles followed, but it would be quicker through the trees.

Her face was lashed by the branches and her legs scratched by the time she burst out of the woods. Ahead of her, the pastures were edged by white fences, which glowed in the moonlight. She saw no clouds of smoke rising from any building, but she didn't slow.

As she neared the house, she discovered the firefighters hadn't gotten there yet. She couldn't smell smoke. Had it been a false alarm? If so, why were the lights off in the house? Had everyone gone to bed?

Impossible! The *kinder* wouldn't return to their rooms quickly in the wake of such excitement.

She heard a muted buzz. Smoke alarms? Where was the smoke? Should she run out to the bunkhouse beyond the barn and alert the stablemen?

Someone reeled across the porch.

"Toby!" she cried.

Running to him, she gasped when she realized he had Mrs. Beebe draped across his shoulder. He eased the cook to the porch, then collapsed himself.

"The...others..." He hung his head for a moment.

"I'll get them."

"I'll help."

"No. I'll do it. Did you see where the fire is?"

He shook his head. "Stay out here. I'll..." He began to cough.

Knowing she couldn't waste time arguing that she was more capable than he was at that moment to help the family, she whirled and threw open the door. She focused her flashlight on the stairs.

No smoke, though the alarms shrieked. Thanking God, she ran upstairs and along the corridor leading to the *kinder's* rooms.

Mia was sprawled across her bed. Sarah couldn't wake her, so she slipped her arms under Mia. The *kind's* head lolled against her chest. Sarah pushed aside her panic. Rushing downstairs, she opened the front door. She placed the little girl on the porch beside Mrs. Beebe. The cook hadn't moved. Toby was on his knees, retching.

Hearing shrill sirens, Sarah prayed for the firefighters to get there as fast as possible. She didn't wait. She ran back into the house. Her head began to spin, and she had to clutch the banister as she came around the top. She saw motion at the far end of the hall where Mr. and Mrs. Summerhays slept, but she continued toward the *kinder's* bedrooms.

She roused Natalie and sent the girl to wake Alexander. Her stomach rocked as dizziness tried to drive her to her knees, but she lurched into Ethan's room. Like his younger sister, he wouldn't rouse. She somehow lifted him and carried him toward the stairs. She felt sicker to her stomach with each step. Clamping her lips closed, she swallowed hard and ordered herself not to vomit. She checked to make sure Natalie and Alexander were behind her.

She wanted to urge them to hurry, but her lips refused to form the words. She waved for them to follow her. When they reached the first floor, Alexander started to sit on the bottom step, but Natalie jerked him to his feet. Putting her arm around him, she lurched toward Sarah.

"Help…" she choked.

Sarah kept Ethan balanced on her hip and put her other arm around his older brother. With Natalie's help, she was able to stumble out onto the porch. Flashing lights seemed to be everywhere around her. Mr. Summerhays was reeling toward the railing, dragging Mrs. Summerhays behind him.

She blinked, but her eyes wouldn't clear. Someone grabbed her elbow and pulled her forward. She wanted to protest that whoever it was needed to be careful. She didn't want to drop Ethan.

Mia! Where was Mia?

"The children are safe," said a kind voice. "You will be, too, once you get oxygen in and flush out the carbon monoxide."

Carbon monoxide?

The words echoed without meaning through her head. A mask was pressed against her face. With every breath she took, everything became clearer.

She was sitting at the back of an ambulance. Inside, two people were smiling as one removed an oxygen mask from a form stretched out on a gurney. She peered through the dim light. The body was too long to belong to the *kinder*. From its height, she guessed it was Mrs.

Summerhays. Sarah sent up a grateful prayer that the *kinder's mamm* was all right.

"Sarah, what are you doing here?" Menno's demanding voice sliced through the cobwebs in her mind but set off a headache that tightened like a heated band around her skull.

"Not now, Menno." The man's voice was familiar.

"George—"

"I said not now, and I meant it."

Sarah forced her eyes to focus on the two men standing in front of her. George, the EMT who had helped Toby, stood face-to-face with her older brother. There was nothing threatening in George's pose, but it also announced he wasn't going to change his mind.

Menno was called away. She didn't see by whom or why, but she was grateful to have to think only of breathing.

George squatted in front of her. "I don't know if you heard me tell you before, but everyone in the Summerhays family is safe."

"What about Toby and Mrs. Beebe?"

"They're going to be fine. Mrs. Beebe is doing the best. She was outside the longest, and she was beginning to recover by the time we got here."

She wanted to ask when she could go and check on the others, but George told her to stay where she was until she got enough oxygen into her system.

The sun was rising over the mountains by the time Sarah felt steady on her feet. She thanked George for his help, then went toward the porch, where Mr. Summerhays was talking with the fire chief. Someone had given Mrs. Summerhays a bathrobe, and she held it closed around her as she listened to what the two men were discussing.

As Sarah walked up the steps, she was relieved to

see the *kinder* with Toby. The youngsters ran to her. She hugged each one, unable to speak through the tears clogging her throat. Strong arms enclosed them, and she looked up to see Toby's drawn face.

"Danki," she whispered.

"If you hadn't come…" He cleared his throat. "You've got a way of always being where you're needed most, ain't so?"

She opened her mouth to answer but halted when she heard Fire Chief Pulaski say it would soon be safe to go in the house because the gas was switched off. They just had to wait while the central air cleared the rooms.

"The problem was your cook was using a stove without a vent—"

"It's being hooked up tomorrow," Mrs. Summerhays murmured.

"She was cooking a brisket overnight, and carbon monoxide built up beneath the pan. The vent would have sucked it out so it wouldn't have been a problem. If Mr. Christner and Miss Kuhns hadn't been here…"

Mr. Summerhays sighed. "I'll make sure it's working before the kitchen is used again. Next time, it could be a fire, which could destroy the whole house."

"Maybe you should worry less about your house and more about your *kinder.*"

Everyone froze. Sarah did, too, when she realized those words had been hers. She pressed her hands over her mouth as every eye focused on her. Out of the faces looking at her, her gaze fixed upon Toby's. Instead of regarding her with shock and dismay, he gave her a nod.

Only he knew how she'd worried about the *kinder* missing their parents and longing for the chance to spend real time with them, not just being showered with gifts or having to make do with a quick conversation when most of the time their parents' minds were on something else. Was this the way God had provided to let her reach out to her bosses and find a way to open their eyes?

"What did you say, Sarah?" asked Mr. Summerhays in an icy tone she'd heard him use once before. That had been when he fired a groom who'd caused a horse to injure itself.

God, put Your words into my mouth so they might reach into the hearts of these parents.

"I said," she replied, "worrying about the house isn't as important as worrying about your *kinder*."

Both parents gasped, and firefighters standing nearby did, too. However, Mrs. Beebe patted her shoulder and Toby gave her a thumbs-up.

"Sarah—"

She interrupted Mr. Summerhays. If she didn't say what he needed to hear, then the *kinder* might never have a chance to have their parents in their lives. "It's not my place to tell you how to raise your family."

"That's the first thing you've been right about. I know your brain must be foggy with—"

"My brain is fine, but it wouldn't matter." She knew she was risking his ire by not letting him finish again. If she lost her job, she needed to do the best she could for the *kinder*. "I'm speaking from the heart. I spend a lot of time with Natalie, Alexander, Ethan and Mia, and I know what's in *their* hearts.

"They're growing so fast, and you're missing it. Natalie wants to spend time with you, Mr. Summerhays. I don't know anyone who loves horses more than she does, and you'd be surprised how much she's learned from listening to you." Turning, she looked at Mrs. Summerhays, who somehow had managed to smooth her hair and look like the cover of a fashion magazine again. "Did you know

Mia sneaks off to spend time in your closet because she wants to be with you? You love clothes, so she believes she can be closer to you by being near your clothes, too."

"I didn't know." Mrs. Summerhays looked dismayed. "I had no idea." Reaching out an awkward hand toward her youngest, she asked, "Do you really do that?"

"Yes, Mommy."

Tears filled gray eyes that were identical in *mamm* and daughter.

"The boys want to spend time with you," Sarah said, not sure how much time she had before Mr. Summerhays lost his temper. "They make mischief to get your attention. The more they have tried and failed to have you notice them, the more desperate they've become."

"I didn't know," Mrs. Summerhays said again. "Children?"

When she held out her arms, the quartet ran to her. They hugged her as Sarah knew they'd wanted to yesterday, and their *mamm* held them close, no longer acting as if her clothes were more valuable than her *kinder*. When she offered her hand to Mr. Summerhays, he didn't hesitate. He bent and waited for his *kinder* to look at him. Ethan was first. The little boy hesitated and glanced at Sarah. When she nodded with an encouraging smile, the *kind* threw himself into his *daed's* arms.

"God works in mysterious ways," Toby said from behind her. "A near tragedy may have opened their eyes to what they could have lost." Putting his hands on her shoulders, he turned her to face him. "They may find change difficult."

"That's why I'm here to help them for as long as they need me."

His eyebrows rose. "Does that mean you're giving up your dream of becoming an EMT?"

She shook her head. "No."

"Your brothers—"

"Don't you think it's time my brothers learned how serious I am about taking the training?" Stepping back, she added, "I do."

"Sarah, you don't have to do this right now." He moved in front of her.

"I think I do." So many things she yearned to tell him, about the state of her heart and how glad she was he'd been in her life, if only temporarily. She had to speak to Menno and Benjamin before her courage failed her.

She walked to where her brothers stood among other first responders. She watched their shocked faces when Chief Pulaski followed her.

"You and Christner made our job easy, Sarah," the chief said, smiling. "Not that I'm surprised. Benjamin and Menno always keep their heads during a fire. I guess good sense and bravery runs in your family. I know it's not your way to put one person above another, but you two are heroes in my book." The fire chief patted her on the shoulder before going to supervise his firefighters as they prepared to leave.

As soon as Chief Pulaski was out of earshot, Menno said, "Sarah, you shouldn't have come here."

"I had to."

"You could have been killed." Benjamin blinked on what looked like tears.

She put a consoling hand on his arm. "You need to know I've got the same yearning that you do to help others. I don't have to have your permission for EMT training, but I'd love to have your blessing."

Menno began, "You're our sister and—"

She didn't let him finish the lecture she'd heard too many times. It would lead to the same argument they'd had before. "You're my brothers, and I love you. I know you worry about me." She let a smile tilt her lips. "Too much sometimes, but you need to trust me to know what is right and wrong. Training to become an EMT won't lead to me planning to jump the fence or cutting my hair and dressing like an *Englischer*."

Benjamin flushed and lowered his eyes. Menno found something in the sky interesting. They avoided her gaze because they'd threatened to do those very things during their *rumspringa*.

Then Menno looked at her. "I've been afraid it would come to this since you took a job for these *Englischers*."

"A job that has allowed us the chance to pursue our dreams. You two have your sawmill because I was able to earn *gut* money as a nanny. I'm going to get the training I want." She took her brothers by the hand as if they were no older than Ethan and Mia. "I believe in you. Please believe in me. This is something I can do."

"But women—"

"I wouldn't be the first woman volunteering in the rescue squad in Salem."

"The first *plain* woman."

"As you were among the first plain firefighters. Someone has to be the first." She smiled. "I know you're worried, but give me a chance to prove to you I belong in the rescue squad as you belong in the fire department."

Benjamin cleared his throat, then said, "She has a point, Menno."

"We promised *Daed* we'd watch over her. Is this what he would have wanted?"

She wanted to shout *ja* but kept her lips clamped closed. Anything she said could make them close their minds again. At least, for the first time, they were being open about why they'd become so protective of her, to the point of breaking her heart.

"We may change our minds," Menno said, "but let's see how it goes."

She stood on tiptoe and kissed Benjamin on the cheek, and then did the same to Menno. When they turned as red as her hair when she was so demonstrative in front of their neighbors, she smiled.

"If you've got concerns," she said, "let me know, and we can discuss them…as *Daed* and *Mamm* used to do. We're a family, and we can't let something one of us does hurt the rest of us."

"When did she get so grown-up?" asked Benjamin as if she were no older than Mia.

Menno shrugged but gave her a rare smile.

Her brothers said they'd see her at home, then went to assist their fellow firefighters. She wanted to cheer her excitement but halted when her gaze locked with Toby's across the yard.

She had a chance at her dream of helping others, but it was a hollow victory when her heart's desire was leaving.

An hour later, with the sun warming the air, Toby rose from the rocker where he'd been sitting, his small bag packed and waiting beside him. He watched Sarah walk across the pasture toward the house. The Summerhays family had gone into Salem to have breakfast at the local diner, the trip to New York City postponed. They'd invited him, so he assumed they had offered to take Sarah with them, too. He'd declined, hoping to spend as much of the time left before J.J. and Ned arrived with her, but she'd gone home to change.

As she climbed the steps to the front porch, she said, "I need to say *danki* again, Toby."

"I heard George say you asked him about when the next EMT training class starts. I guess that means your brothers are okay with the idea."

"I couldn't have stood up to them if I hadn't known you, Toby Christner."

"I just told you about the women being EMTs in other settlements."

She shook her head hard enough to make her *kapp* bounce. "You did so much more. You helped me see what I do makes a difference."

"How could you have doubted that? Look what you've done for the Summerhays family!"

"No more than you did."

He caught her face between his hands and gazed into her eyes. How he wanted to lose himself in their sweet warmth, to swim in them and never worry about leaving again. That wasn't his family's way of doing things. They were leavers. Arrive, create a big to-do and then leave without cleaning up the mess.

"No," he whispered, trying to memorize every inch of her lovely face, "I mean, what you did before this morning. You made those *kinder* believe their dreams could come true." His voice grew husky as he whispered, "Even if you continued to believe yours couldn't."

"I never doubted that."

"You never believed those dreams should be put first. You were ready to stand aside and let everyone else's dreams—including mine—push yours aside. I'm sorry, Sarah. I don't know if I can ever be the man you need. A man who can set down roots. It's not the way Christners do things."

"You aren't your *daed* and *mamm*. You're you. Toby Christner."

"Who has been so careful not to let moss grow beneath his boots."

"You've stayed on J.J.'s ranch for years."

"I've worked for him for years, but as soon as the chance came to travel while delivering horses, I jumped at doing it."

"Of course you did, because you care so much for the horses you train. You were anxious for them to make a *gut* transition to their new homes."

Was she right? Could he be unlike his parents? If there was anyone in the whole world he was willing to change for, it'd be Sarah, but to try and fail would hurt her far more. That he was sure of.

The rumble of a big truck came from the long driveway. He prayed it was Summerhays, bringing the family home, but he recognized the powerful engine.

J.J.'s truck!

He lifted his bag.

Her face crumpled, and he realized she'd clung to the hope that he'd stay. He couldn't speak, because saying goodbye was impossible. Instead, he walked to the truck.

Sarah remained on the porch. He saw her flinch when he closed the passenger door. She waved half-heartedly when J.J. called a greeting before putting the truck into gear.

Toby's gut told him he was making the biggest mistake of his life, but he knew if he loved Sarah—and he did—he couldn't take the chance of subjecting her to the miserable life his *mamm* and he had endured. As the truck drove toward the road, like his *daed*, he didn't look back.

Chapter Seventeen

The week before Christmas, the large family room was redecorated in a style approved by the four Summerhays *kinder*. Unlike the flawless decorating magazine decor that once had seemed to shout "Stay out!" the room reflected—at last—the family who lived there. A huge sectional and chairs, looking well used, were arranged to offer a view of the enormous fieldstone fireplace with its crackling fire and the large flat-screen TV hung next to it. Books and video games were scattered over once pristine coffee tables. Photographs of the *kinder* were displayed throughout the room.

In one corner in front of a large bay window, a tree from the newly named Kuhns Family's Christmas Tree Farm held court. It was definitely not a designer tree, because it was covered with handmade ornaments and strings of popcorn and cranberries. Ornaments made of homemade dough were painted with food coloring. Others had been decorated with pasta or glitter. So much silver tinsel covered the tree it was almost impossible to see the greenery. Softly falling snow drifted past the window behind its branches.

From the ceiling, crepe paper in bright shades of red

and blue were twisted and draped from each corner to the center of the room. Someone must have found an extra box of Christmas tinsel, because silver strands hung from the garlands to reflect the light from the pair of crystal chandeliers. A big sign hung over the fireplace where a nativity was displayed on the mantel. Both *congratulations* and *graduation* had been spelled wrong by the *kinder*, who'd wielded the bright orange and blue markers and still wore the colors on their hands.

A cut-glass bowl, filled with red punch being kept cold by rainbow sherbet, had been placed beside a sheet cake with the same words on top of it, but correctly spelled. The guests, *Englisch* and plain, mingled with a sense of familiarity and friendship that grew out of being neighbors and from working together in the Salem volunteer fire department.

Sarah hadn't expected Mr. and Mrs. Summerhays—or Ian and Jessica, as they'd asked her to call them in the wake of the near disaster—to throw a party for her upon her graduation from her EMT training. They'd insisted it was the least they could do for the woman who'd saved their family. Because Sarah suspected they meant more than when she and Toby had dragged the family members out of the house, she'd acquiesced.

The past three months had brought astounding changes to the Summerhays family and her own. Maybe because her brothers saw her training was as important to their fellow firefighters as to her. They treated her again as an equal in their household, making decisions with her. As for the Summerhays family, many trips had been cancelled so both parents remained at home more. Ian and Jessica seemed amazed at how much they enjoyed their *kinder*.

Alternating between "thank you" and "*danki*," Sarah

let the guests know how much she appreciated them coming. She hugged her friends from the Harmony Creek Spinsters' Club and shared the evening with her fellow graduates from the EMT course. The Summerhays *kinder* raced about, playing with their plain neighbors. They'd become fast friends since; many of the parents in Harmony Creek Hollow had, with a bit of help from Miriam, changed their minds about the *kinder* playing together. Ian had invited the scholars to enjoy softball games in his unused pastures.

"Congratulations, Sarah," she heard yet again. This time from behind her.

Sarah started to turn and respond but couldn't utter a word as she stared into Toby's intense blue eyes. She couldn't mistake them for others. Glancing down, she saw he once again wore cowboy boots, a sure sign his ankle was healed. Snow was melting off the shoulders of his dark coat.

"You're here!" she whispered.

"I am," he replied, once again the terse man he'd been when they first met.

Tears rose into her eyes. They splashed along her face as the man who'd filled her dreams even before she met him stood in front of her.

"You're here for my graduation party?" Even saying the words out loud didn't make it seem possible that Toby had returned from Texas.

"For that and other things."

Her battered heart ached as hope died within it again. She'd heard Ian talking about a new horse he was expecting to be delivered. It must have been coming from J.J.'s ranch and, again, Toby had joined his boss in bringing it north. How soon would he be leaving again?

When his broad hand cupped her chin, she was shocked

he'd be so brazen in public. It wasn't the Amish way to show open affection, even when a couple was walking out together.

Then again, Toby Christner was unlike any other Amish man she'd met.

"I had to see you again," he said, his voice as rough as his skin. "Our farewell felt wrong."

"And you want to get it right?" She hated her sarcasm, but she was mixed-up. She loved him. If he'd come back to say goodbye again, she wasn't sure her heart could bear it.

"There are a lot of things I need to get right." His thumb traced her cheekbone as he tilted her face so she looked into his eyes. They stood that way for a long minute, then he took her hand and led her out of the crowded room and into the entry hall.

Nobody followed them, and he didn't stop until they entered the fancy room where they'd first waited for Ian to arrive to talk with J.J. He released her hand but didn't move away from her.

As if there hadn't been a break in their conversation, he said, "Sarah, you know I've spent most of my life avoiding getting involved with people in order to keep from getting hurt. In doing that, I cut myself off from myself, too, to the point I forgot how to laugh until you gave me a reason to again." He gave her a wry grin. "Does that make sense? It did when I heard it in my head, but saying it out loud…"

"It makes complete sense." She laced her fingers together in front of her apron to keep from reaching out to put her arms around his shoulders. "Has that changed?"

"Before I answer your question, I think you should ask another one. You haven't asked me how long I'm staying this time."

"I don't want to know that. I'm enjoying the blessing of having you here right now."

"Ask me."

"Why? The party—"

"Please, Sarah, ask me."

Though she had to fight to push each word out, she tried to keep her voice light as she asked, "How long are you going to be here for this time, Toby?"

He took her hands again and laced his fingers through hers. "For the rest of my life."

"What?" She was sure she'd heard him wrong.

"Your boss has offered me a job. He advanced me enough money to purchase a few acres along Harmony Creek. I plan to build a house and become a member of the *Leit* here."

"You do?" This had to be a dream. The sweetest dream she'd ever had. "J.J.—"

"Is happy because he knows I'll be here to train the horses he breeds, and he'll have Summerhays Stables as a customer for years to come." He drew her to him. Letting her hands go, he slipped his arm around her waist. "Sarah, how can I leave you after you've taught me how important it is to be connected to others and to God?" His fingers swept along her cheek again, sending tingles zipping through her. "How can I leave the one I love? We hadn't even reached the main road before I knew I had to return here to ask you to be my wife."

"You've been gone for three months."

"I had to follow your advice." He brushed a strand of hair back toward her *kapp*. "You told me before I left that I needed to forgive my *daed*. You were half right. I needed to forgive him *and* forgive myself. It took me two months to find out where my parents were living." He shook his head. "Believe it or not, they've found a settlement that suits them. It's not like any plain settlement I've ever seen because there's constant debate about everything, but they love it. When I saw how happy they were, forgiveness came easily."

She folded his hand between hers and squeezed it. "The Lord has blessed you."

"He's blessed all of us. When I finally listened to my *daed*, I discovered he'd been looking for a place where he thought my *mamm* and I would be at home. Somehow, he found it for us." His grin widened. "The day I was ready to leave my parents' house, Summerhays called with a job offer, and I knew God approved of my plan. Will you marry me this Christmas, Sarah? You've made Summerhays and his wife realize they want to be a real family, and you've made me realize I want you and me to be a family, too."

She couldn't answer because four young voices were shouting, "Toby! It's Toby!"

The Summerhays *kinder* poured into the room and rushed to throw their arms around him. Sarah stepped back to give them space. She laughed when they all talked at once, asking questions, telling him about what they'd been doing, urging him to try the cookies they'd baked for the party.

Toby gently peeled Ethan and Mia from his legs and set them back a step. He patted the older two on the shoulders before saying, "I've told you a bunch of times that you need to listen and give Sarah a chance to answer before you ask more questions." The *kinder* looked puzzled, until he added, "Let's start by having her answer *my* question. Will you be my Christmas bride, Sarah?"

Excited squeals came from the youngsters, but Sarah looked only at Toby.

"Ja," she said, unable to stop the tears tumbling out of

her eyes again. "*Ja*, I want to be your wife. I want us to be a family." She laughed. "You'll be my Amish Christmas groom in every meaning of the word."

"Finally! Someone got it right and knows I'm not a cowboy." He gave her the grin that caressed her heart, the smile she knew he shared with nobody else.

"I don't care what you call yourself as long as you're mine. *Frelicher Grischtdaag*, Toby."

He wished her a Merry Christmas, too, before his laughter warmed her lips as he claimed them in a kiss that thrilled her to the tips of her toes.

Shouts of more congratulations drew them apart, and Sarah saw her brothers leading the cheers. She leaned her head on Toby's shoulder, knowing her most precious dreams were coming true.

* * * * *

If you enjoyed this story,
pick up these other stories from Jo Ann Brown

Amish Homecoming
An Amish Match
His Amish Sweetheart
An Amish Reunion
A Ready-Made Amish Family
An Amish Proposal
The Amish Suitor

Available now from Love Inspired!

Find more great reads at www.LoveInspired.com

Dear Reader,

Family...

The most important people in our lives are our families. Some are related by blood. Others come into our lives in different ways. They're the people who matter the most, the ones we'd risk anything for...and the ones who drive us crazy at times. We get the angriest at our family because what they think and do and feel matter deeply. Like Sarah and Toby, we have to learn to understand and forgive our families, something that can be more difficult than forgiving friends or strangers. We must come to see that what annoys us is coming from a place of love, a place where we are truly blessed.

Visit me at www.joannbrownbooks.com. Look for my next story in the Amish Spinster Club series, coming soon.

Wishing you many blessings,
Jo Ann Brown

"I've got trouble, Clarabelle."

The cow didn't answer her. Bethany pitched a forkful of hay to the family's placid brown-and-white Guernsey. "The bishop has decided to send Ivan to Bird-in-Hand to live with Onkel Harvey. It's not right. It's not fair. I can't bear the idea of sending my little brother away. We belong together."

Clarabelle munched a mouthful of hay as she regarded Bethany with soulful deep brown eyes.

"Advice is what I need, Clarabelle. The bishop said Ivan could stay if I had a husband. Someone to discipline and guide the boy. Any idea where I can get a husband before Christmas?"

"I doubt your cow has the answers you seek, but if she does I have a few questions for her about my own problems," a man said.

Bethany spun around. A stranger stood in the open barn door. He wore a black Amish hat pulled low on his forehead and a dark blue woolen coat with the collar turned up against the cold.

The mirth sparkling in his eyes sent a flush of heat to her cheeks. How humiliating. To be caught talking to a cow about matrimonial prospects made her look ridiculous.

She struggled to hide her embarrassment. "It's rude to eavesdrop on a private conversation."

"I'm not sure talking to a cow qualifies as a private conversation, but I am sorry to intrude."

He didn't look sorry. He looked like he was struggling not to laugh at her.

"I'm Michael Shetler."

She considered not giving him her name. The less he knew to repeat the better.

"I am Bethany Martin," she admitted, hoping she wasn't making a mistake.

"Nice to meet you, Bethany. Once I've had a rest I'll step outside if you want to finish your private conversation." He winked. One corner of his mouth twitched, revealing a dimple in his cheek.

"I'm glad I could supply you with some amusement today."

"It's been a long time since I've had something to smile about."

Don't miss
An Amish Wife for Christmas *by Patricia Davids,*
available November 2018 wherever
Love Inspired® books and ebooks are sold.

www.LoveInspired.com

Get 4 FREE REWARDS!

We'll send you 2 FREE Books plus <u>2 FREE Mystery Gifts.</u>

Love Inspired® books feature contemporary inspirational romances with Christian characters facing the challenges of life and love.

FREE Value Over **$20**
